PECKHAM'S MARBLES

Sue:
Happy Birthday 1988
Love

al

PECKHAM'S MARBLES

PETER DE VRIES

McGRAW-HILL BOOK COMPANY
New York   St. Louis   San Francisco
Toronto   Hamburg   Mexico

Reprinted by arrangement with G. P. Putnam's Sons

First McGraw-Hill Paperback edition, 1987

1 2 3 4 5 6 7 8 9 **ARGARG** 8 7

ISBN 0-07-016650-1

LIBRARY OF CONGRESS CATALOGING-IN-PUBLICATION DATA

De Vries, Peter.
Peckham's marbles.

I. Title.
[PS3507.E8673P4   1987b]   813'.52   87-2730
ISBN 0-07-016650-1 (pbk.)

The public does not make exquisite distinctions.

—G. B. Shaw
in a letter to G. K. Chesterton

I

ONE

"The last place to have a ball, my dear Mrs. DelBelly, is at a formal dance. Or such I myself have found to be the case."

The chief obstacle to Peckham's progress with Mrs. DelBelly lay undoubtedly in his inability to chew the rag, or fat. He could never seem to get the hang of it. Or having got it, he'd lose it, succumbing in the end to his besetting vice, the "art of conversation" as practiced by a few and feared and resented by the rest of us. He and Mrs. DelBelly would be chatting cozily, say, about the passing of the flyswatter from the American scene, when he would dilate on "a nostalgic artifact once a staple of every household." Who needs it? Blooey would go their momentary rapport. Or they would be chewing the fat about the peculiar waddle Mrs. Peptide had developed since going to her podiatrist, when Peckham would explain walking as a regulated fall and recovery of the locomoting biped, bringing *that* subject to grief. Once, God knows how, they got on the topic of shoofly pie, where and when they had eaten or at least seen it, etc., and Peckham began a discourse on references to the dessert in American literature, and from there it was a learned little tangent on foodstuffs as they figured in the work of Wolfe, Proust and Joyce, till the breakdown in communications was again complete. There is nothing wrong with wanting somebody else's money if erudition through no fault of your own has left you broke and friendless, or fluency in retailing it has stood you in as much social stead as ring around the collar. A girl had once broken an engagement with him because he couldn't talk United States. Now here he was at Dappled Shade, trying to make a socially acceptable sow's ear out of the silk purse that was Earl Peckham, long enough to win Mrs. DelBelly's heart—and, yes, her money. She had wanted it herself when it had been young Frank DelBelly's; it had become her own when they married, and even more so when he died and left her a widow; and now it was to be safeguarded from fortune hunters who hadn't two nickels to rub together but could work their mouth pretty good.

His very first day as a patient at Dappled Shade, convalescing from a bad case of hepatitis, Peckham had spotted Mrs. DelBelly as a woman not radically his senior— say fifty to his forty-odd—who, though inescapably large of frame, carried herself with something like regal style. In fact a debate raged within himself whether he should tell her she reminded him of a Wagnerian *Heldinsoprano*, about to give out with the *Liebestod* after each deep-bosomed breath. And casing her in further detail, he learned that she wasn't really an inmate of the sanitarium but its principal owner, taking a few weeks' lodging here while her nearby house was done over from stem to stern, and also to root out certain financial irregularities she had heard were undermining the profits. Thus one could not say she was as ample as her means without by the same token saying her means were as ample as she. Discreet inquiries revealed they were of divergent faiths. She was an Episcopalian, Peckham a Dadaist. But who could say that in this era of ecumenism the two denominations might not soon one day merge? Meanwhile, seventeen rooms (according to rumors) and five baths admit of the most elastic conceivable definition of compatibility. With that much space, two people could drift apart and hardly notice it.

Meals at Dappled Shade were not taken at rigidly assigned tables. You got your eats cafeteria-style and then sat down wherever you wished or could. Not exempting herself from this participatory democracy left Mrs. DelBelly's society prey to anyone, but few presumed on it, least of all Peckham. Not appearing to hog her company was at least half the impression he tried to create of deserving it. He did slip into the last remaining empty chair of her table-for-eight at dinner two days after their abortive little shoofly-pie chat, held on the grounds on a warm July afternoon. The occasion was not auspicious for his resolve to commit no flights into the abstruse.

Present with them was a local music critic in for a nervous breakdown following a traumatic failure to understand a noted musicologist's widely circulated judgment of a new Czech composer. He called him "the Stravinsky of music." Try as the critic might to grasp this arcane mot, its meaning eluded him; nor did the quantities of friends and acquaintances who shared his bafflement assuage his crisis—after all, he was supposedly an authority and should be dispensing exegesis, not asking it, sometimes from people buttonholed in public; once, in fact, on the street, such was his extremity. He had accosted an old man with wild-flying gray hair, seen hurrying out of Avery Fisher Hall at Lincoln Center. The old man had shaken his head in the negative on hearing the query. " 'Karpaty Talcum is the Stravinsky of music.' No, I have no idea what it means," he'd said, and gone his way, possibly troubled in spirit himself, to telephone and buttonhole acquaintances of his own in a chain reaction of bewilderment. Some intimates of the critic, whose name was Bruno Sweltering, professed to understand the oft-quoted paradox, but their elucidations proved kinkier than the original and only left Sweltering worse off than before. Now and then as he flogged his brains to understand it he thought he had its meaning, but then it would slip from his grasp like a bar of bath soap from your fist. Doubts that he was a fit member of his profession vexed nights already insomniac enough. His fixed idea was diagnosed as an idée fixe. A period of rest was prescribed, and so here he was at Dappled Shade, in the particular care of Dr. Auslese, whose prognosis was "fair for a return to normal life, poor for a resumption of his vocation."

In spite of it all, he laughed a lot with steadfast teeth, probably to keep his spirits up while his guts rotted in self-doubt. The eight at Mrs. DelBelly's table talked about an upcoming concert at the nearby Westchester Bowl. It would be an all-Delius program, which gave Sweltering a chance to get off a few zingers of his own. "At least the mosquitoes will fit right into, hmm hmm, his peculiar brand of tonality, mmbahahaha," he said. Peckham nodded brisk agreement, holding a finger aloft to indicate that a concurring comment would be forthcoming, directly he had swallowed a wad of lasagna. He touched his napkin to his lips and said, "I find Delius rather mucilaginous, and of a certain lachrymosity." Sweltering bobbed his head in assent, but Mrs. DelBelly rolled her eyes at the rest as if to ask how anybody capable of such inhuman literacy was allowed to run around loose. Of course Peckham wasn't doing that exactly, was he, running around loose? Still, in a few weeks he would be at large in society again, free to spread pain and consternation on a plane with the Talcum business, given his story that he was here only on a nursing-home basis after a bout of hepatitis, which she secretly doubted. That she had not consulted the files to which as proprietor she had free access was to her credit as a lady. "It's none of my beeswax" had been her honorable rejoinder to Mrs. Peptide's hint that she take a peek at Peckham's folder or press Dr. Hushnecker for details.

To change the subject, Mrs. DelBelly deplored her unbridled consumption of the lasagna even as she lifted a dexterously burdened fork to her lips, adding that anyone with a weight problem should avoid pasta of any kind, in a manner that invited demurrer. Which Peckham was more than ready to give. "Nonsense. There are people lean as myself with pots, while someone with the right skeletal frame for it can carry off any amount of weight. You came through that door like a galleon under full sail."

15

All of this led to his overhearing her remark later to Mrs. Peptide, with whom she was thick, "He has no small talk."

Well, they would see about that!

That Mrs. Petptide's own small talk was all she had, and that submicroscopic, a moment's eavesdropping behind a clump of rhododendrons the next morning sufficed to confirm. The two women sat on the lawn just beyond his protective screen, in a choice corner of the beautifully groomed grounds, holding a conversation that certainly qualified as chewing the fat. He listened carefully a moment to get a good fix on how it was done according to their lights, because he definitely planned to join them as a way of advancing his cause with Mrs. DelBelly. The cost of that might be a half hour or so of Mrs. Peptide's twaddle. He would show that he could descend to a level of easy colloquial familiarity without a sacrifice of such intellectual endowments as must, simultaneously, make him a good catch. That was the ticklish combination to be orchestrated here. Just as he squatted down so his head wouldn't be visible above the foliage, Mother Nature strolled by, expecting as usual to be complimented on the day, if not the season.

"Quite the most beautiful July I've seen in years," Peckham said. "One of your best."

"Oh, thank you," Mother Nature said, fluttering a blue chiffon hanky the same color as her dress, a very full-cut gown that fell in easy folds about her own ample body. "So glad you like it," she added, and continued on by. Peckham returned to his eavesdropping, cocking an ear sidewise against the broadleaf foliage, and even into it.

"I had an ingrown toenail on my left tootsie, this one

here," Mrs. Peptide was jabbering away. "On the foot thumb, as Dr. Bledsoe calls it. And he fixed it up just by taping the flesh tightly *away from the nail where it was cutting through the skin*. Could have done it myself and saved twenty dollars."

"Still in all, he may have disinfected it or something, so you wouldn't get like a felon on it. So it may have been a double sawbuck well spent," Mrs. DelBelly said. "That was one of Frank's expressions. He had a great knack for slang usages, for all his being a figure to be reckoned with in better textiles."

Peckham popped erect and materialized through a cleft in the shrubbery, grinning richly, like an illusionist making himself appear from nowhere. Ta da.

"Masticating the old suet, are we?"

That was not good. The two women stared at him blankly.

"Mean to say, chomping the proverbial tallow?"

Again zilch. The women turned to look at one another as though seeking instruction from each other, some clue as to how this might best be dealt with, but all either did was clear her throat uncertainly. Peckham made a third and final try for comprehension, a last attempt to click.

"Spending the summer morning noshing the well-known adipose? Gumming the time-honored fabric?"

They looked at him as though this was where he belonged. Right here at Dappled Shade. Plenty of fresh air, wholesome food, regular hours—oh, something to make him sleep of course—and two sessions a week, maybe three, with either Dr. Hushnecker or Dr. Auslese.

Mrs. DelBelly, who had a way with animals and hard

cases, famous for it, took matters in hand. Her reigning principle: a little humor sees us through. Can get us over the roughest or around the toughest situations.

"Well, what you don't meet when you haven't got a gun," she said, again drawing on one of her bygone hubby's store of quips and ploys. Anything to break the ice, just be careful not to fall through it. "Sadie, I don't know whether you've met Mr. Peckham. Mrs. Peckham, Miz Peptide."

"Who could meet Miz Peptide and not remember her," Peckham said, seizing on the "Miz" as though they were all idiots drawling the hot summer days away in a Southern gothic novel in which no one had ever done anything all his life but chew the rag. *He would be grasped.*

He glanced suggestively at the single remaining free chair, occupied by the women's handbags and a wad of knitting stuffs. They politely removed them, Miz DelBelly taking the yarn and needles into her lap and resuming work on something apparently destined to become a yellow scarf. The needles flew, as though she were trying to forget as soon as possible Peckham's latest spout of jabberwocky. "Why, thank you kindly," Peckham said, surprising himself with an adverb he normally loathed, and lowering himself with a neighborly "Ahh" into the slatted wooden seat. "One always finds Adirondacks surprisingly comfortable once one has sunk into one and forgotten the way it looked. Which is like something rather devised as an instrument of torture, or some newfangled chiropractic exercise, don't you agree?"

"We spent our honeymoon there," Miz Peptide said, to

keep the conversational ball rolling, however downhill.

"Not wholly in one of these, I trust!"

"No, the mountains. They're simply beautiful. They take your breath away. You have to believe in a Supreme Being."

"I'll remember that when and if I marry," Peckham said with an arch glance at Miz DelBelly. She was wearing two dresses of dove gray, or so it seemed from the long matching tunic covering a main undergarment. A supple acquaintance in the designing game had once told Peckham that women of volume deliberately dressed tautologically, as though to show they had nothing to fear. The willowy bloke had written a book entitled *A Thing to Wear* and was forever to be seen on the telly chat shows. *He* knew how to chew the rag, granted it was all silks and satins being munched away at.

"You've just come," Miz DelBelly said. "Will you be with us long?"

"Alas, no. I'm only here to rest, a spell in dry dock, you know, after a rather nasty siege of infectious hepatitis. We nearly lost me."

"I'm glad to hear that. That we didn't, I mean," Miz Peptide put in. God knew what she was in for. Probably just a case of midlife rattles.

"That was one of Frank's expressions," Miz DelBelly said with a gentle smile. " 'Dry dock,' for being sick in bed. Tell the boys at the office they've got me in dry dock for a while. Nothing serious. Be back Monday."

"I take it, from the tenderness with which you recall it, that Frank is your late husband," Peckham said. "I

19

count it an honor to possess even so slight a fragment of similarity with one who, having married you, must have been one of the most fortunate of mortals."

"Well, thank you. You're very sweet."

"Of course being in dry dock like this for so long does give a fellow the blues." No harm in applying for a little sympathy. Peckham didn't amplify on his melancholy's being traceable to the enforced denial of alcohol, a prohibition remaining in force for another good month. He readied a nifty that had scored more than once before, though he himself was sick to death of it, like an actor delivering lines however freshly stunning to new audiences. "Nothing like a bout of hepatitis to make a chap look on the world with a jaundiced eye."

Again zilch.

"Well, the fresh air and good food here will soon get you in apple-pie order," Miz DelBelly said.

"She naturally plugs the place," Miz Peptide said. "She's not here as a patient, she owns the place, and is giving it a good look-see while her house is done over."

"Oh, is that so?" Peckham said, feigning ignorance of facts he had already thoroughly cased. He returned to the subject of himself. "It all works out fine for me. I'm on sabbatical from the university where I've been teaching." This was bending the truth more than a little. He had left in a huff after being denied tenure, that in turn resulting from his failure to attract students to his elective seminars. His creative writing course had been a special problem. Two years before, his enrollment had dwindled to one. And last year it had fallen off a little.

"What do you teach?" Miz Peptide asked.

"In addition to one course in creative writing, I've had others in American literature, mostly contemporary. Hemingway, Faulkner, Dreiser, the usual lot. Last semester I taught Henry James."

"And was he a good student?"

"Smart's a whip and bright's a dollar."

He was doing it! Chewing the rag! He was getting the hang of it. So much so that he even dared hope he might confidently ask Mrs. DelBelly to go for a moonlight walk. He envisioned ripening acquaintance, familiarity, then at last sufficient intimacy to ask her to marry him. Of course it would probably be a marriage of convenience in the classic sense, he providing her some cultural ambiance in return for the unclouded leisure in which to hammer out a sequel to his recent novel, *The Sorry Scheme of Things Entire*—whose fate in the bookstores more than substantiated its obvious premise. It triumphantly bore that out beyond all cavil! Peckham's present post-hepatitic languors made him quite content with the idea of a platonic union; and yet, given complete recovery, he might not be altogether past singing the body electric, nor Mrs. DelBelly herself not totally past rating it. Comparison with the younger Mrs. Peptide certainly made her steadily more palatable. Her square face, while neither beautiful nor pretty, was definitely handsome, etched with lines as few as the gray strands in her brown hair, and her large eyes were the color of Vermont maple syrup, maple syrup held up to the sun. They sparkled when she laughed, a fine complement to her white teeth. An influence more elevated than she was probably used to might make her truly blossom on all counts. His own eyes were known to have been called no less than Svengalian. One woman had left him because she felt she could no longer be herself under his steady suzerainty. Who was to say Mrs. DelBelly would prove any less malleable under masculine thrall? More than once in the perhaps ten minutes they had sat together now he had sensed her raising her eyes uncomfortably to his own gooseberry gaze. That had been Alicia's term for the ever-piercing scrutiny that had made her flee for her life.

"Frank, God rest his soul, was a self-educated man," Mrs. DelBelly said of the man who had given her his name. "Never got past high school, but could you tell it? Huh! Not a bit of it. Did a lot of his reading at night, though not necessarily the sets of classic authors he stocked our library with. Or let some decorator put in for us. Let them go uncut while he pored over books he bought about explorers, his favorite. His specialty. Devoured everything he could about Columbus. That was natural, being as how he was Italian himself. His dedicated obsession, rather than a mere hobby. His hobby was collecting old peroxide bottles."

"Columbus has always rather fascinated me too," Peckham said. "A most complex and interesting character. One of the greatest navigators of all time, but put him on dry land and he was completely at sea."

Mrs. DelBelly nodded over her flying tines. "He knew how to handle people, from Queen Isabella to the sailors. He would often falsify the log to quiet their superstitious fears, keep from having to turn back and all would be in vain."

"All often is, but we must not despair." She might take some doing. Revision would not be easy. But that very fact promised the excitement of a challenge, when that of the chase itself had run its course. "Give him this continent and he thought it was the Indies." Peckham persisted in what he knew was a fruitless attempt to salvage the gag. "When he had blundered his way down to Cuba, he thought it was China. It was of course the greatest serendipity in history. Our reaching Mars and thinking it to be Venus would be roughly the parallel for all time."

"Space is our last frontier," Mrs. Peptide's own glandular composition made her say. He was glad he wasn't going to marry *her*. He had chosen wisely.

"Well, it's been most pleasant chewing the fat with you," Peckham said after a few more minutes, hoping the emphasis he gave the key term would clear up any confusion remaining from his original gambit which, while bang-up, so he thought, as Wodehousian pastiche, could be seen in retrospect as bewildering to folk of middling endowments. "But now I see my English publisher has arrived. He's taking me to lunch."

"Oh, you have an English publisher?" Mrs. DelBelly asked with the first definite show of being impressed.

"Oh, yes."

This was bending the facts rather a goodish bit. It was true only in the sense that his American publisher happened to have been British-born—he hadn't an English publisher at all, and only a slim hold on an American one. Dogwinkle could be seen making his way across the walk with something under one arm and something else in the other hand. Being "taken to lunch" had sunk from expectations of being whipped into town in the rented car Dogwinkle had been driven out from New York in, and a meal at something like the Algonquin, down to a picnic on the lawn here at Dappled Shade, and that picnic not from a handsome wicker hamper but from what turned out to be a shoebox full of peanut-butter-and-jelly sandwiches. The thermos contained enough hot coffee to see them through a dessert consisting of a choice between Hostess Twinkies and Devil Dogs. Dogwinkle *loved* this country.

"Then we shan't see you at luncheon here," Mrs. DelBelly said. So she was a shan'ter. Whether that was good or bad in her case remained to be seen. Would bear watching. Oh, the insanely fine line between the O.K. and the de trop!

"No, alas. Which makes me look forward all the more eagerly to dinner. Potluck company has been mostly luck for me." Mrs. DelBelly smiled in a manner suggesting that a pretty compliment intended as such had been so taken. Then she said, "What college do you teach at?"

"Windsor, a place in Wyoming."

She lit up. "Wyoming! I had a grandfather there. He was a minister in the Presbyterian Church. Preached to the cowboys, going from ranch to ranch on horseback. In fact he preached on horseback very often. Traveling from place to place like that I guess it was always the same sermon."

"Sort of the sermon on the mount, you might say."

"Well, I doubt he was that good. Hardly in the class with our Lord."

"No, I meant because it was on horseback. The *sermon on the mount?*"

Mrs. DelBelly's ball of yellow yarn had fallen from her lap, and Peckham quickly stooped to retrieve it from the grass. "Thank you. I guess delivering it so often, week after week, Grandfather had it polished to a fairly well, but I doubt he would invite comparison to our Savior. Well, we mustn't keep you."

Peckham had seen Dogwinkle standing hesitantly on the steps of the main building, gazing uncertainly around, and now made himself known with a wave and a shout. He took leave of the ladies with a courtly bow, expressed the hope that he would see them at dinner, and struck out across the lawn toward his cheapskate of a publisher.

On the way he again ran into Mother Nature, who again expected a compliment of some sort, so he murmured a word of congratulation on the beauty of the sky. "I'm so glad you like it," she answered. His onward passage took him past the gravel turnaround, where the driver of the rented car was leaning against a front fender, munching one of the sandwiches, a can of Coke in the other hand. He probably expected to hear bursts of maniacal laughter or see one patient emptying water from the sprinkling can on another patient's head, if not catch a glimpse of an orderly with a net pursuing a runaway. People strolling placidly toward the main building in response to the luncheon bell no doubt disappointed him. He watched quizzically as Peckham joined Dogwinkle.

"Jolly sorry to have to do it this way," Dogwinkle said, setting the thermos down to shake Peckham's hand.

"But I explained that some of us are perfectly free to get away without any signed permission or anything. I could have popped into New York and met you at—"

"No trouble at all, I assure you, old boy. Nice drive, and—Ah, hullo, here's a spot just being vacated by your lady friends." The two women joined the dribble of inmates converging on the front steps, leaving Dogwinkle free to drag a nearby table over and settle it between two of the Adirondack chairs, into one of which he sank gratefully. He uncovered the shoebox, the lid of which at least read "Bally," and proceeded to take out sandwiches wrapped in wax paper which, spread out, served as plates and place mats both. He snicked a dead moth miller from the table onto the grass and sighed contentedly. "What a relief from the metropolitan rat race, to say nothing of the Algonquin, Lutèce, one stuffy cluttered haunt after another when one's blood cries out for the open sky and the clean air."

"I've never been to Lutèce, and as for—"

"I know you like peanut butter and jelly. Mentioned it often."

"But only as a boyhood staple we were so stuffed to the scuppers with that now the very thought—"

"Needn't sell me, old chap. I've become quite a convert to that plebeian American delicacy of yours. Amazing how many gustatory gems are assembled from unlikely combinations. Apple pie and cheddar cheese, now who would

26

have thought they would marry well and live happily ever after? Toffee and apples on a stick, of all things. Melon and prosciutto."

"That's not one of ours, and if you never had p-b-and-j's in England, all I can say is, you've lived a sheltered life. I've run into them more than once in London."

"I remember you took your Java with cream and sugar. Lots of sweets, I suppose, for the duration of your alcohol ban. When my brother had hepatitis I remember they stuffed him with candy bars till he couldn't see straight."

Peckham watched Dogwinkle pour coffee into two cups, one a collapsible metal thing conjured from a corner of the shoebox, and the other, for himself, the unscrewed top of the thermos.

"Cheers. And may it soon be martinis we'll be lofting anew. No more ardent wish was ever uttered, my dear Peckham. God bless."

Peckham was going to say "Call me Earl," but his tongue became mired in a wad of peanut butter which itself cleaved to the roof of his mouth.

Dogwinkle settled his heavy blond bulk more comfortably into his chair and drew a document from his breast pocket.

"I promised you the sales figures for the first half-year period. They're not jolly numbers, mind, but then we both always knew *The Sorry Scheme of Things Entire* was something special. Not for the old lady in Peoria, as you say here, and will it play in Dubuque and all that sort of thing."

"It's the old lady in Dubuque and will it play in Peoria."

"Right. To date, *Sorry Scheme* has sold— Let me see

27

here." He unfolded the statement and scanned its contents, humming and clucking his tongue with what seemed miraculous ease, given the nature of their meal. "Dum de dum . . . da do dum dum . . . Ah, here we are. It's sold three copies."

"Three."

"Quite."

"As of?"

"June thirty. Date the first semi-annual statements go to. Of course we're now in mid-July, but I doubt we can expect much of a rally. Three is probably it."

"But they'll stick. I mean they won't come back."

Dogwinkle shrugged and tucked the statement back into his pocket. "Too early to tell. It's after the holidays that the returned copies usually come pouring in. Bookstores tend to keep them till Christmas business is over. Homing-pigeon time, we call it at Dogwinkle and Dearie. At least we won't have that with *Sorry*," he added a wry smile. "A flood of returns."

For some obscure reason Dogwinkle had also taken a ballpoint pen from his pocket, and when he tried to replace it he dropped it, and the few moments he was fishing it out of the grass gave Peckham a chance to lob the rest of his sandwich over Dogwinkle's head into the shrubbery behind him. It got caught midway its descent through a rhododendron and remained tangled in the foliage there. Peering into the open shoebox, he saw that for dessert there was the choice of Hostess Twinkies and Devil Dogs. At the Algonquin, Dearie, the other partner, would be feeding poached salmon with *sauce vert* and white aspar-

28

agus to Poppy McCloud, whose bestselling bilge presumably made it possible for the firm to "bring out" writers with something to say, while at Lutèce his, Peckham's, agent was unfolding a six-figure contract for a woman with powdered shoulders whose gothic-romance crud similarly subsidized authors whose books were not intended for people with a wad of sealing putty between their ears.

"*The Sorry Scheme of Things Entire* isn't a very catchy title, after all, is it?" Dogwinkle said, pocketing his pen at last.

"The *Rubáiyát* has been mined for so many successful titles that I figured . . . I mean *The Wine of Life*, *Some Buried Caesar*, *The Same Door*, *Some for the Glory*. To say nothing of *Ah, Wilderness*. And you yourself turned down *Paradise Enow* for a title."

"I mean for a collection of essays."

"*Sorry Scheme* isn't a collection of essays."

"It isn't?"

"No. It's a novel."

"I'll be damned. Didn't have a chance to read it myself, you know, it was recommended by a reader whose judgment I trust implicitly (who cried, by the way, when I showed her the statement). I figured when the report said 'existentialist vein' it was a philosophical sort of treatise, with relevant modern overtones. You don't expect a book like that to set any Guinness records, but I mean three copies. Another sandwich?"

Peckham shook his head, glancing apprehensively but by no means guiltily at the one lodged in the shrubbery, like the ram in Abraham's thicket. He bit into the Hostess

29

Twinkie, which tasted surprisingly good, as did the coffee.

"One of those—the three—is a copy I signed over to the bookstore in town here." The "over to" was a locution he remembered from years in the Middle and Far West, a cozily colloquial replacement for "over at" that was rag chewing at its most quintessential best. "Do you have any idea who ordered the other two? Could you find out?"

Dogwinkle laughed, not unkindly. "Why, do you want to autograph them as well, so they can't be returned? We'll then be assured a solid 'No Returns' on this title all right, what?"

"Why, what do you mean?"

"Can't return inscribed copies. Been defaced. Lose their consignment status."

Where Dogwinkle had picked up this bit of misinformation would be an interesting question, but picked it up he had, and with it sent any number of authors from store to store, eagerly offering to sign any stock on hand, in the delusion that its royalties were safe from all harm. Peckham's resolve was also instant. Given the name and address of the store or stores that had taken the other two copies on consignment, he would hunt it or them down if it took his last nickel, and autograph the books with a vengeance.

They munched their dessert treats for a bit, gazing about themselves as at a day not to be missed. "Lucky to get, say, twenty like this a year," Dogwinkle said.

"I saw by that *Times* story the other day you're giving Poppy McCloud an advance of a million two."

"Oh, but you see that's for the next three books, and the thing people, other writers, don't realize when they read about those whopping advances is that they're against all earnings, including the author's share of book clubs, paperbacks and whatever. That settle the adrenaline down a bit? Look at that sky."

"I couldn't read *Break Slowly, Dawn,* hardly even past the title, but thanks for sending me a copy."

"Oh, those pop romances aren't your dish of tea. Surprised anyone in our office sent you one. Waste of postage. But you must know yourself, old man, that it's bestsellers like her who make it possible for us to publish more— subtle stuff like yours. Even a book of verse now and then, though you can't get poets to grasp that. The Hilary Hinkles of this world look down with utter contempt on its Poppy McClouds. But she doesn't return the compliment. Knows she's a potboiler. I sent her *Sorry Scheme* and got back a nice note saying she enjoyed it. Are you working on something else?" Dogwinkle asked apprehensively.

"Few thousand words into something. Getting into dry dock slowed me down a bit."

"Title yet, might one ask?"

"*Palestrina's Toenails.*"

"In the antiromantic vein of the hour, eh? Look, if you could, I mean just a weeny concession here and there—"

"I haven't settled definitely on the title yet. I'm also thinking of *This Muddy Vesture.* From 'this muddy vesture of decay,' you know."

"Dear. Mean to say, if you could see your way clear to lightening up just a weeny bit. Give people a ray of hope." How Peckham hated that word *weeny,* especially from a man. Now he became remorseless.

"It's about a crippled nine-year-old girl who's run over

31

by a truck and killed on her way to her piano lesson, just when she's learned to cross one hand over the other on the keyboard to the delight of her simple-minded Hungarian parents, who have scrimped and saved to give her the opportunities they themselves never had," Peckham went on, less because the book was about any such thing at all than out of a desire to give Dogwinkle no quarter. Whereby hung a tale.

It had been in boyhood that Peckham had first divined he was cut out to be a writer, in no small measure because of a gift for metaphor early given notice of. Like the time, at the age of ten it must have been, when he told his mother that when he was really mad at something or somebody he felt "like my Boy Scout knife with all the things pulled out." Not a bad figure of speech for someone bristling with antagonism—as he was now with Dogwinkle. Him and his Scout-hike sandwiches piled like Pelion on the Ossa of the sales figures for *Sorry Scheme*, which alone should have sent the firm into penance for their failure to spend a thin dime on advertising. Carping about the title only added to Peckham's vexation. Yes, he was abristle with all his blades out—except possibly for one. The knife itself remained safely sheathed, owing solely to Mrs. DelBelly as a prospective presence in his life, a mood-suffusing thought counterbalancing his pique even now. That qualified his emotion, by no means enough to cancel out his anger, mind you, merely soften it. He would not harden his heart absolutely against Dogwinkle. Dogwinkle did not merit actual wounding, only a bit of a pinking with, say, the screwdriver attachment, or the corkscrew (not to beat the metaphor to death). But yes, Dogwinkle must be punished.

So it was with a pleasant smile that Peckham said, "Your name. I've always found it intriguing." Christ, how he hated that word. It had always been *verboten* in any class of his. "Anyone who uses the word *intriguing* in this course, orally or on paper, will be flunked," he invariably announced at the beginning of term. His inadvertently blurted use of it now was further evidence of how Dogwinkle had rattled him. There he sat erect even in an Adirondack chair, stocky enough but all muscle. There were rumors in publishing circles that he was proud of his plank-flat stomach.

"Actually it's the name of a seashell," he said. "Your government issued a stamp on it recently. Twenty-two-center. Picture of the so-called frilled dogwinkle on it. You may remember it."

"Of course, now I do. Very charming little seashell. Always nice to recall how we're all descended from the sea, our primal Mother. One of the women you saw talking to—saw me talking to a while ago is called Mrs. Peptide. Probably originally oceanic in its implications too."

"Well, that's to do with amino acid groups, I seem to remember from chemistry class. Peptide is the name for these compounds or something. Bit rusty on the subject. Not, of course, that her name comes from any such at all. Some other origin altogether, word garbled or something. I mean, what would possess a scientist to call amino acid *compounds* that?"

"Maybe there was a professor among her ancestors who

discovered the compounds and gave them that name."

"Could be. We had some neighbors named Caterpillar. And there's this Peeperkorn character in *The Magic Mountain*. Look, this has been really fun. I hope you're on your feet again real soon." Dogwinkle climbed to his own. "I'll leave these goodies for you. No, please, I mean it, including the thermos, with another cup of coffee for you to dawdle over in lieu of the brandy we both ardently wish we might have topped it all off with. The minute they let you off the wagon you let me know and we'll tip over a bottle of the old bubbly."

As they shook hands across the table, Dogwinkle said, "Deuced if I can remember the exact passage from the *Rubàiyàt* our title's from. So it won't nag a bloke all the way back to town, can you recall it?"

Looking Dogwinkle straight in the eye, except for one moment when Dogwinkle flicked his cowed gaze away and may very well in that instant have caught sight of the sandwich caught in the rhododendron, Peckham recited the entire verse:

> "*Ah Love! could thou and I with Fate conspire*
> *To grasp this sorry Scheme of Things entire,*
> *Would not we shatter it to bits—and then*
> *Re-mould it nearer to the Heart's Desire!*"

Dogwinkle looked a bit shattered to bits himself as he withdrew his hand, firmly retained in Peckham's grasp till the absolute end of the recitation, as though aware not only of the ironic applicability of the title to the fate of the book itself, but of his firm's guilt in not promoting the volume any better than it had, even in the face of reviews reading "one of our less abrasive minimalists" and the like. Dogwinkle and Dearie were themselves part of the Sorry Scheme of Things Entire, was what Peckham's piercing Svengalian gaze tried to convey—and in large measure must have done, judging by how Dogwinkle's own eyes tried to avoid it by dropping like two grapes from a rotting cluster, and then by the chastened aspect with which Dogwinkle with his teeny this and spot of that turned and hurried across the grounds to where his car was waiting. That the p-b-and-j's too had their incontrovertible place in the Sorry Scheme of Things Entire might sink in on the ride home, somewhat tarnishing the sybaritic pleasure of being whisked back to his office in a rented limousine—*also* paid for by the Poppy McClouds of this world if it came to that. But Peckham cranked out some gratitude for the visit nonetheless, however much of a gad it was for Dogwinkle.

"Thanks a million," he called as Dogwinkle made toward the car. Dogwinkle half swiveled about and waved acknowledgement without breaking stride. Peckham stood watching him, his expression now turning somewhat sardonic. "Make that a million five!" he shouted. But the amended figure was lost under the sound of the car door clapped shut by the driver as Dogwinkle sank into the back seat with a well-imaginable sigh of relief, for the ride back to town.

TWO

Last night he dreamt he went to Manderley again. But instead of the iron gate briefly impeding Rebecca's passage in the bestseller of that name as well as in the movie made of it—Peckham's favorite Hitchcock—what appeared to obstruct Peckham seemed a comparably formidable width of privet, as though he were trying to enter the palatial preserve from the side. He crashed through it like a runner carrying a football across the line of scrimmage, to confront a backfield not of foliage but consisting solely of the oblong battle-ax to whom Joan Fontaine was a paid companion in the film. But the identity was only ephemeral. She dissolved cinematically into Mrs. DelBelly. With that adroit pirouetting twist valuable to broken-field runners he foiled an attempt to tackle him, the resulting success curiously mingled, however, with the sense of having been frustrated in an attempt to tackle *her*—an ambiguity typical of dreams. Further complicating that was Dogwinkle's sudden replacement of Peckham as her adversary; or rather (again characteristic of the duality in dreams) their being telescoped together as combatant-suitor. Then it was Peckham alone facing Mrs. DelBelly with bared teeth across a width of fabric, a rag to chew, the length of which was an infinity along which they must gnaw their way for a stretch of time itself apprehensible as an eternity. In other words, this was hell.

What vexed Peckham's waking recollection of the dream was his inability to recall the name of the actress cast as the tartar to whom Joan Fontaine was a paid companion, until spirited off by Olivier to an even worse fate at Manderley. A dependable Hollywood heavy. Florence something . . . ? What a thing to flog your brains with in the dead of night. Wasn't the laudanum hour bad enough without such trivia left as flotsam by dreams like that?

"You looked very cozy with your English publisher there," Mrs. DelBelly remarked when she and Peckham sauntered together about the grounds that evening. He had contrived to accidentally merge their moonlight strolls after some reconnaissance from the veranda. "I remarked to Miz Peptide that you could have had a pass for lunch off grounds. I'd been glad to arrange it myself. I mean you're not *that* . . . What goodies did he bring you?"

"Oh, picnic stuff, you know. Some pâté, a little caviar, cucumber sandwiches." He wondered whether she had seen him stuff the shoebox and thermos into one of the wire litter receptacles distributed about the property. "And peanut-butter and jelly as a concession to what I am afraid is my ofttimes rather plebeian taste." He must chuck the "ofttimes" sort of thing. That was for friends who knew you well enough to realize its mock quality. "Call it my culinary slumming. Brings back Boy Scout days. Were you ever a Girl Scout?"

"Oh, yes. Up from the Brownies. We all remember peanut-butter-and-jellies very well. No picnic without *them*."

"Or overnights, slumber parties. All that. I remember my kid sister 'flying up' from the Brownies to the Junior Girl Scouts. Isn't that the way it goes?"

"Yes. You fly up."

Temporary flight was something for which Peckham would have been grateful now, for they were approaching the trash basket in which the remnants of the picnic lunch still lay, fully exposed in the bright moonlight. But by skipping a step ahead of Mrs. DelBelly and then as subtly drawing back abreast of her he managed to keep it out of her line of vision. Seeing it still unemptied might have made her complain as chief owner, even rummage about to investigate its contents, like a bag lady. That was not to be ruled out, as she ran a tight ship here. He nudged her along a fork in the path that would guarantee a different return route. The gravel crunched steadily under their rhythmic footfalls.

Mrs. DelBelly raised her eyes rapturously to the sky, along which creamy white clouds blithely scudded.

"For some campfire outing each of us Girl Scouts had to render a selection, and mine was the speech from *The Merchant of Venice*. 'How sweet the moonlight sleeps upon this bank!' "

The Chase Manhattan, Peckham thought, by way of a natural association against which he was powerless, where a few of my pitiful securities toss and turn in the deepmost vaults, while your far more ample ones rest in peace celestial as this. He immediately reproved himself as churlish in admitting the thought, one typical enough of this—

39

how did the speech end?—this muddy vesture of decay which doth grossly close out the something or other harmony in immortal souls and something still quiring to the young-eyed cherubins. They were neither of them that!

"When a woman gets to be my age she's more grateful to the moon than the sun."

"Nonsense. You're a woman of great fiscal attraction."

Jesus Christ! Had he actually said that, or had the of course intended "physical attraction" fallen like that on his inner ear? It may very well have come out as such in this day of sloppy diction. He often deplored his own slipshod enunciation no less than that of his students. His unconscious may have been playing sly tricks on his conscious, but not he on Mrs. DelBelly, let God judge. A pretty compliment had been intended and, obviously, so taken.

"Well, thank you."

"I meant it. There's a line in one of Scott Fitzgerald's books—"

"My niece is always reading him, and spouting him to me. But no matter, spout away. It's a perfect night for it."

"Yes. I don't even recall the exact book, but something about the moon being up to its old work of covering the world's bad complexion. Your complexion certainly needs no such cosmetic favors. You must know it's one of your best features. Smooth as a baby's . . . "

"A baby's what?" she laughed, sensing the proverbial comparison at which he had shied.

"Nothing. Just a baby's."

"Liar, liar, pants on fire. That's what we used to say as kids."

"We too. Look, I don't mean to pry, but I happen to have this crowbar on me. The question naturally arises in the case of a woman so beautifully in her prime as you. Do you wish to marry again?"

"Oh, yes. Absolutely. I firmly intend to."

Peckham was timing the duration of their silences by counting their gravel crunches, noting, with the compulsion of the obsessive neurotic, those that were synchronized and those that were not. This particularly pregnant silence went twenty-eight crunches, eighteen of them in synch, allowing for his hopping a step now and then to readjust his pace to hers. He wanted to walk in unison as much as possible.

"Give us a kiss."

The grating of their footsteps ceased as Mrs. DelBelly stopped cold in her tracks with a gasp. Again she looked at him as if he belonged here, either (a) permanently, with any off-grounds passes issued over her dead body, or (b) temporarily, while a sterner retreat better capable of handling dangerous lunatics could be found, including potential or actual sex cases. He was almost as surprised as she. The words had simply popped from between his lips like a cork from a champagne bottle, with no really rememberable act of volition behind them. In a way they were part of or the product of a trance through which he could detachedly observe them both floating, as in a kindred fragment of the recurring Manderley dream, or as temporary occupants of a misty Ingres nocturne through which they jointly drifted, two more poor wards of the immemorially deranging moon.

"Have you gone completely buzerk, Mr. Peckham?"

41

"Call me Earl."

"I'll no such thing, but I may call you a lot of other things, besides calling the security guard."

"I'm so glad to hear you say that, because it touches on my explanation." He laughed reassuringly, in a manner intended to pooh-pooh all fears away. "You see, I'm writing about a character I have say exactly what I just did, under circumstances not dissimilar. I've been stuck with the question of what the woman's reaction might be, and therefore I deliberately popped it to see what yours would be. Now I know what she'd say, because she's a woman somewhat like you. A woman of parts, of substance. A stout representative of middle-class values," he said. "What makes the circs the same," he went on, using one of Mrs. DelBelly's pet abbreviations that markedly qualified his ardor, "is that the scene occurs in a park, which in a sense this is, and she might very well summon a guard! So you see. Are we good friends again, with me forgiven for making a guinea pig of you? You must admit I said it with a certain jocosity."

"Jocosity schmocosity," Mrs. DelBelly said, with such telling effect that Peckham could only exclaim "Touché!"

"Touché schmouché," Mrs. DelBelly returned, repeating her triumph with a force that left Peckham with no comeback whatever. She flounced away and resumed her walk with such a quickened pace that Peckham had to run to catch up with her. There was nothing to do now but go for broke.

"Give us a kiss. This time I say it sincerely. I mean to press my suit."

"You might get it cleaned while you're at it, too. It's nuts like you who give mental hospitals a bad name."

"Now it's from the heart, which I freely give you." He enacted a pantomime of literally proferring her his still-beating organ in cupped hands as they hurried along, Peckham doing his best to get in front of her so she could see his dramatic business. Mrs. DelBelly for her part performed a scene of tearing her arm from a grasp in which it was not in fact being held. The gesture, too, was purely symbolic, meant to imply that making a pass at her was by no means something she would put past him. The jerk was preventive.

"And you call yourself a Christian," Peckham said, sustaining the cupped-hands attitude as one might find it in a statue of the Lord in whom she professed belief. She glanced down, as though at the hands of a mendicant begging alms in a flea-infested marketplace. Then she broke into a real trot, Peckham following suit to keep abreast of her, so that to a distant observer—and indeed there was one, in the form of Mother Nature watching from another walk—they might have seemed like a happy couple out for an evening jog. "The seh . . . second time is also in the story I'm wuh . . . working on," he puffed. "You've guh . . . got to believe me. A writer must have ver . . . verisimilitude or his work is nothing. You know that as a wide reader. So there you have the whole thing."

It was a quarter-mile of serpentine walks before she cooled down, slowing gradually, like a racehorse after crossing the finishing line, and breathing heavily, her bosom heaving, as one of Dogwinkle and Dearie's bestsellers might have put it. Peckham was by this time even with her, his hands no longer a chalice containing his bleeding heart but hanging at his sides.

"There. You see how we can blow things up out of proportion? Eh? Everything okaykums now?"

"I suppose I did overreact."

"Pshaw. We all do it. And you did catch a fella when he's feeling a bit tempest-tossed," Peckham said, switching to the little-lost-boy approach available when the Svengali one was temporarily not in working order. He waved vaguely toward the main building from which support could be summoned for his claim to sympathy. "Sit, Jessica," for they had reached a park bench, offering an opportunity to effect a charming revival of her *Merchant of Venice* recitation memory.

"Look how the floor of heaven is thick inlaid with patines of bright gold," she took nostalgically up as she seated herself at one end of the bench. He settled himself discreetly at the other. She had so far cooled down as to be warming up, enough, at least after a few words of apology from Peckham, to apologize herself, and make amends for her reaction by inviting him to a party she was giving to celebrate the completed restoration of her residence. Since it was an open house, it hardly rated as an invitation, but then. "It's a week from Sunday. Will you still be here?"

"With bells on. You pick up the lines with such natural grace that your name might well be Jessica. Just what is it, as a matter of interest?"

"Nelly. Rhymes sort of too well with my last name, but

then that wasn't it when I was christened. I was an Aspenwall."

"An" Aspenwall. Then there were "the" Aspenwalls, from the sound of it. Money begetting money, as of old, and to be with us world without end. Still, he repented conjuring the Chase Manhattan as the bank the moonlight sweetly slept upon. The bathos had been rather untypically perverse of him, really, not a true measure of his venality.

"I shall be so glad to come to your party, as I'll be leaving shortly on an autographing tour."

"Oh, really. That sounds glamorous. Though I'm told they can be grueling. Pop you from one city to another, to say nothing of TV interviews they arrange for authors on those promotion trips. How many cities will you hit?"

"I'm not entirely sure yet. Not many."

Peckham had definitely resolved to learn exactly what stores had bought the other two copies of *Sorry Scheme*, seek them out, and inscribe them, come hell or high water. At least he would have a perfect record of no returns— something few authors could boast. There were wretches who had them come home to roost by the tens of thousands. Dogwinkle and Dearie could remainder the bloody remainder for all he cared—which would of course be tantamount to the whole damned forlorn and misbegotten first and last edition. But this satisfaction he had obsessively planned.

"So I'll be delighted to have your housewarming as my last pleasant memory of Westchester ere I set out."

Peckham felt he had matters reasonably in hand after a narrowly averted disaster when he set out for the housewarming on the appointed Sunday evening, one as balmy as could be hoped. And it was as he traversed the gravel walk to the Tudor mansion awaiting him that the name of the actress playing the harpy Joan Fontaine worked for in *Rebecca* popped into his mind. Florence Bates. That was it. Why did he think of it now? It was an interesting question, as what wasn't.

THREE

God save Peckham from tastefully furnished rooms. It was no doubt his nausea with the term itself, evoking as it did a pussyfooting care for things that "went well" together. "Motifs"—areas "done" in French provincial or Chinese Chippendale—gave him the particular willies. One great gulp of a look at Nelly Aspenwall DelBelly's enormous main parlor showed it to be no such featureless monochrome devised by a hired decorator. It was a warm and comfortable assemblage of objects clearly bought one by one because each had somewhere somehow taken her fancy. Here was a refectory table probably encountered on a Mexican holiday and shipped home. There a mirror found poking around in a shop in Barcelona. That fringed shawl on the grand piano may have been picked up in the Wisconsin Dells. Oh, the cerulean blue of the walls was probably an idea of the professional esthete hired to oversee the restoration, and possibly held in check by a meat-and-potatoes carpenter with both feet on the ground, and the former had no doubt had a hand in selecting the fabrics in which the chairs and couches had been reupholstered, as well as whatever wallpapers might lie in wait upstairs, once the promised grand tour was under way. But the whole breathed an air of frankly eclectic preference—to the extent that it could be discerned through, around and beyond the sixty or seventy people sitting and standing about with drinks in their hands. Peckham found himself inadvertently humming "Hail, Bright Abode" as he threaded his way among his hostess's happily admissable conglomeration toward an especially long sofa with an empty place on it beside Dr. Hushnecker.

Hushnecker confirmed the ballpark figure, with the assurance that it would swell by the minute. A circulating waiter fetched Peckham a virgin Mary with commendable speed, with which he clinked glasses against Dr. Hushnecker's own Scotch and soda. From where he sat, he could look into the adjacent library, stocked with sets of the standard authors, as one could tell from the fine bindings. One could spend a honeymoon here, cutting pages Mrs. DelBelly had admitted Frank had left unviolated in preference to biographies of explorers and the like with which he spent much of his spare time. Another name refusing to surface began to plague Peckham. What Frenchman was it again who, when asked who France's greatest poet was, answered, "Victor Hugo, alas"? Would he be nagged half to death trying to remember *that* now? Both authors no doubt sat embalmed in half-morocco there, in that snug retreat.

"Everybody and his brother here," Dr. Hushnecker observed of the crowd now spilling over into adjoining rooms, including the library. "Or should I say everybody and her husband. It's surprising the number of men who eventually turn up at parties 'wild horses couldn't drag them to.' Mean it when they say it too—'I hate cocktail parties.' Why does everybody hate cocktail parties and then willingly go to them? Stick around till nine, ten o'clock when the hosts want to dump the ashtrays and get the dishes stacked in the sink, and off to bed."

"There's an old saying," Peckham replied. "Misanthropy is a plant that like any other requires nourishment, and is best fed by socializing. The misanthrope requires gatherings such as this to fertilize and water his dislike of his species, while, alternatively, the self-sequestered can safely nurture his de facto affection for the race by chronically absenting himself from it, as Unamuno has emphasized in his confessional on precisely the subject, and thus the two polarized elements in the oxymoron complement each other by canceling one another out."

"I don't believe I've ever heard that saying," said a woman seated in a nearby chair who had been listening to the conversation. "Is it Chinese? They usually are."

Peckham was trying to frame a serviceable reply to that when the woman popped out of her chair with a happy cry and went over to greet a newly arriving friend, leaving the field to Dr. Hushnecker. He said:

"Have you had any therapy before coming here?"

"Oh, a visit or two. Nothing much. Nothing in what you call depth."

"We might reinitialize it."

"You mean start over again?"

"Yes. I know you're just at Dappled Shade on a con-

49

valescent basis. Rest home, and I hope it's been that after your nasty ailment. Mrs. DelBelly tells me you're going on a whirlwind autographing tour. All very fine, but I pin little hope on the 'change of scene' treatment for the kind of depression Dr. Auslese and I both know you've been in."

"You're quite right. We have an old saying where I come from. *Weltschmerz* is hardly cured by travels about the world of which one has grown weary, though doubtless here and there some faith might be pinned on the practice of homeopathic remedy sometimes somehow inherent in the contradiction."

"Is that what they say where you come from? Where is that?"

"Wyoming. We have any number of such folk saws that, I might say, stand us in good stead in our back country."

One of the catered waiters wandered by with a tray from which fresh drinks might be plucked or on which empty glasses might be set. Dr. Hushnecker traded his empty glass for a fresh Scotch and soda, and Peckham did the same with his virgin Mary after making sure the replacement was innocuous. They both took large gulps and settled back as they were.

"Last night I dreamt I went to Manderley again."

"*Again?*"

"Except that this time I dreamt I was dreaming it."

"Not an uncommon experience. What do you suppose all this Manderley business means? I've seen the movie, and of course remember that opening line, which you say is the same as the novel's. Refresh me on the iron gate business."

"It bars the heroine's way at first, and then melts away, giving her access to a house not too much unlike a ruined version of this, probably. The gate stops me cold too, then gives way. Melts."

"Your personal version of the frustration principle experienced by every dreamer in one form or another. Often the barrier doesn't give way, or changes into something else, depending on the sleeper."

A free association with the word *sleeper* as referring to a work of art that unexpectedly takes off from cult respect to commercial glory, was safeguarded from Dr. Hushnecker's prying curiosity, as was Peckham's vexation at being barred even from cult kudos, no less than from the six- and seven-figure advances shoveled into the coffers of blockbuster hacks who couldn't hold a candle to him. As was also the fact that in his dream the barrier was sometimes Mrs. DelBelly. What if the good shrink knew of his dreams of conquest there!

"Well, Doc, is Mr. Peckham giving you a busman's holiday?"

Mrs. DelBelly stood before them—Peckham flatly rejected the description "towered over them"—in a flowered housecoat that eluded flamboyance by the liberal sprinkling of leaves among the blooms, and by the loose, Matisselike modernity of the flowers themselves. They did not take themselves seriously in a representational sense, had in fact an offhand, slapdash quality revealing again something in Mrs. DelBelly's innate taste that snatched her from decorative ruin. The gown's neckline offered the discreetest minimum of cleavage, and her hair was swept upward into a spiral as much at the top of her neck as at the base of her skull. The skin had the ivory smoothness of a peeled elm wand, and she was again a sight all the more toothsome for the teeth. But —"Doc"? Could the name for him be a pet romantic one, or was it a familiar term for a man after all a business associate. An employee, if it came to that.

Peckham tried to squelch the sudden fear of a rival by deliberately conjuring an image of intimacy between the two the better thereby to laugh it out of court. Hushnecker's walrus mustache and equatorial waistline ruled out amorous conjuction as grotesque. But then most people's imagined coupling seemed that to Peckham. There had never been any real question of his climbing aboard Mrs. DelBelly, only of a companionship in the financial security of which he could write whatever sequels to *Sorry Scheme* he still had in him.

"Do sit down with us, Nelly. You can circulate later." Peckham quickly scooched over so as to leave space between him and Doc into which Nelly could lower herself— would by the demands of courtesy have to lower herself, rather than sit on the other side of Doc, an arrangement Doc had slyly tried to contrive until foiled by Peckham's counterscooch. So there they all were, wedged in together as Doc said, "Mr. Peckham is going on this whirlwind autographing tour you say, Nelly."

Mrs. DelBelly said: "I happened to be in New York a few years ago the day that bookstore just below Bergdorf's, Doubleday, had an autographing session for Tennessee Williams, whose I think autobiography had just been published. Well, so help me Hannah, the line was out through the door, down Fifth Avenue and around the corner of Fifty-sixth Street. I went in to get something else, a mystery in the paperback section downstairs, I believe, and there he was, sitting in state at a table, gracious as you please, while the customers came on, and on, and on. Biggest formal autographing they ever had, the manager told me. Let's hope you draw crowds like that on your barnstorming trip," she finished, giving Peckham a jab in the ribs with her elbow and making that chucking noise out of the side of the mouth that is uttered both by farmers to make their horses giddyup and by more urban people as a way of implying "Hot stuff." Her intending encouragement did little toward taking the edge off her making the sound, which grated on Peckham even when star movie actresses did it, and which, when added to the "So help me Hannah," tended momentarily to cool his ardor. What infinitesimal details are storm warnings of unsuitability! Perhaps she should be reevaluated as matrimonial timber. Entire chapters of his books were studies in such grating minutiae.

Convalescence from hepatitis is by no means steady. The most euphoric illusions of returning pep can be suddenly reversed by feelings of fatigue, and the languor by which Peckham was now visited without warning was only deepened by the realization that the other two had begun a chat about a local bridge club to which they both belonged. Peckham welcomed exclusion from it, truth to tell. He hated cards. Oh, he liked a friendly game of solitaire now and then, over a brandy nightcap or some such, but the tensions of competition and even of partnership over a rickety folding table were too much for an introvert of his grain. If the bridge-club gossip percolating on his left was a measure of Mrs. DelBelly's interest in that game, then Doc could have her. It could be another straw in a mounting suspicion that he would have to dump her. Leaning his head back, he closed his eyes and smiled at the memory of a cherished grandfather who, as a card fanatic, had the same exclamation for every hand dealt him. "Hoo boy." It made no diff (another of Mrs. DelBelly's regrettable contractions) whether the hand was good or bad, and so the reaction was the equivalent of a poker face. Indeed, he had the same ejaculation for everything— a breathtaking view, a Thanksgiving turkey, a car stalled with a broken fan belt, a "fulfilling" woman. "I spent a week with her in Petoskey, and hoo boy. Ah, hoo boy."

Shouldering the demands of sociability once again by at least opening his eyes put in Peckham's direct line of vision a finely crafted young girl in a red dress, churning her way voluptuously toward the chow line. "Hoo boy."

"What?" This from Hushnecker, who seemed all the while to have assumed Peckham's at least peripheral inclusion in the bridge-club chat. Peckham slid erect. "Nothing." Good God, had he murmured it aloud in his abstraction? "I was just noticing the sumptuous buffet. Mrs. DelBelly is certainly doing us proud."

Watching the line form, he remembered the last time he had heard the old man deliver his familiar exclamation. An elderly couple in the lengthening queue prompted this shift in his reminiscence. Peckham had been visiting his grandparents in their Arizona retirement village, some years before. Both were then plagued by arthritis and other such wintry afflictions. They spun out their days in a kind of companionate infirmity. There seemed an appointed hour for each one's bath, Granny's just before supper, and one evening they excused themselves to see to it together, Grandfather's ministrations being evidently required for her. Sipping his sherry in the parlor, Peckham could hear sounds of water running and splashing, and occasional gentle laughter. It was a good quarter hour before they rejoined him, both glowing pink from their exertions. As the old man sank onto the sofa beside Peckham, he turned with a touching little smile and said, "We used to take showers together. Now we help each other in and out of the tub." He gave a puff of exhaustion. "Hoo boy." The familiar exclamation had never come out in quite that way.

Peckham felt a sense of disturbance at once vague and keen. He had never taken a shower with anybody. Could any significance be attached to that? Current fiction (except his own) as well as movies galore seemed to regard collaborative shower-taking as common, and even obligatory, amorous practice. Yet his modest but by no means negligible handful of affairs, two of them near marriages, had been devoid of any such Dionysian romps. Was that his fault? Evidence of some kind of inhibition lurking behind the intellectual façade of emancipation? Had his several escapees found him in the end a bedroom pooper, not up to larks that had figured in even his grandparents' repertoire? It was not too late to mend his ways. He would turn over a new leaf. He would reform. He would become

a hedonist. Taking a shower with the first opportunant (if
there was such a word) was put at the absolute top of his
erotic agenda, the very next of the rosebuds to be gathered
while he might. That would seem to clinch the rapidly
forming resolution to drop Mrs. DelBelly, whom you could
probably not wedge yourself into a shower stall with and
quite close the door behind you. She would no doubt fill
it to capacity herself, not that by so musing you were by
any means ruling out Rubensesque amplitude as one female
glory. But with time's wingèd chariot at your back you
must act as promptly as possible on a vow so made.

The girl in the red dress was just then moving toward
the buffet spread, and with Nelly off circulating, subdi-
viding herself among her guests as the hostess in her put
it, and Doc otherwise engaged, Peckham popped to his
feet and hurried over in hopes of coinciding with her at
the table there.

Midway his broken-field dash toward his goal, he was
stopped cold, indeed quite like a football runner able to
slither and swivel his way just so far through the opposition, by an obstruction consisting of Mrs. Peptide and two
people with whom she was chatting, and to whom she
insisted on introducing Peckham. One was Father Tooker,
a local Episcopal priest, the other a Mrs. Spinelli, the
housekeeper, taking a few minutes' respite from the strains
of supervising the band of hired caterers. Mrs. Peptide's
synopsis of the conversational story thus far took Peckham
somewhat aback, considering its source.

"We were just discussing whether God has a sense of
humor," she said, then told the other two, "Mr. Peckham

has opinions on everything. Don't you, Mr. Peckham?"

"Everything but that."

"We're not even sure Mr. Peckham believes in God," Father Tooker rather jovially put in, after a sip of sherry.

"Only in a most susceptible one."

"Susceptible?" Raised eyebrows.

"To an infinity of definitions."

"Ah." Eyebrows down. "I like that. But it's getting us off the subject, which is whether God has a sense of humor. Oh, of course we read in the Old Testament about how he that sitteth in the heavens will laugh at kings and rulers who have got out of line, and will hold the nations in derision, and one thing and another. But it doesn't answer the basic question, which hinges squarely on whether he would be amused, say, by the 'Who's on first?' routine, or get a bang out of Perelman's 'I have Bright's disease and he has mine.' Would that—to boggle at nothing essential to the question—would that draw a boffo from the Almighty?"

This grotesquely unexpected topic tongue-tied Peckham, but not so Mrs. Spinelli. "It'd have to," she said, for emphasis tapping the empty metal tray she was holding.

"Why do you say that?"

"Because they say—*you* say, Reverend—we're made in his image. O.K. If that's the case, then he has to have humor, because humor is such a basic part of our makeup. Listen to all the cackling and yacking going on around us now. Can hardly hear yourself talk. If God has no humor, then we're not made in his image. On the other hand, if he does, well, it gives you the willies to think of being

57

governed by a Divine Being who'd split a gut over what's-
his-name's joke you just cracked about Bright's disease.
I've got to go see to the buffet table," she said, and van-
ished, leaving them with a dilemma worthy of the hair-
splitting scholastics of the Middle Ages.

Father Tooker gave a low whistle of amazement. It was
an amazement Peckham quite shared, though for a different reason. It had nothing to do with profundities hidden from the wise and prudent and revealed unto babes
and sucklings, and all that, but arose rather from his sense
that Mrs. Spinelli seemed much too mirthless a sort to be
interested in the subject of humor at all, let alone whether
it was a character constituent in the Most High. Her
face—he had taken fleeting note of it before as she threaded
her way among the guests—wore a perpetually dour
expression, more to be associated with a Scotch Calvinist
than an Italian Catholic, which inquiry proved her to be.
There was something secretly brooding, even festering, in
the dark eyes, which handsomely complemented the olive
complexion of her oval face. Fine figure too for a woman
obviously in her forties. Shapely legs, and hips that swayed
nicely in locomotion. Peckham's glance in her direction
as she made away enabled him to take in the fact that
Red Dress had also been buttonholed by somebody, making this delay with Father Tooker a help rather than a
hindrance in his plan to coincide with her at the chow
line. With Mrs. Peptide headed for the food herself, the
two remained locked in an intricate extension of a subject
Father Tooker was quite keen to pursue.

"The whole question of laughter is fascinating in itself,"

he said, after another sip of his sherry. "Every thinker seems to have taken a crack at analyzing it. Why do we laugh, as human animals?"

"That's hopeless," Peckham said. "Nobody knows why we laugh. Period. What we laugh *at* lends itself somewhat more gratefully to analysis." He flicked an eye again at Red Dress to make sure her detention warranted a little more filibustering. She was clearly having her ear chewed off by a bore she was visibly chafing to get away from, so he must hurry. "Aristotle's thesis seems to me still the most cogent."

"And what might that be? Do fill me in."

"That we laugh at that which, if there were more of it, could cause us pain."

"Example."

"Your Perelman gag lends itself perfectly to the Aristotelian theory. 'I have Bright's disease and he has mine' is funny. 'I have Alzheimer's disease and he has mine' isn't. Goes over the line into the painful. Law of diminishing returns has operated. But both jokes have the same comedic core."

"Ah, I see, said the blind man. We laugh at a man slipping on a banana peel, but not if he fractures his skull and has to be rushed to the hospital. By George, I'm tickled to death to have run into you—Peckham, is it? I'd like to pick your brains some more on the subject. You see, I intend to preach a sermon on it, that's how it came up originally. Mind if I steal some of your stuff?" the clergyman asked with a laugh.

"Help yourself. Any—Oh, I see someone flagging me,"

Peckham fabricated, seeing Red Dress on the loose again. "It's been nice talking to you, and hope we meet again soon. If you'll excuse me. See you in church," Peckham threw over his shoulder, and scuttled across the room in time to land squarely beside the target female at the end of the chuck line.

She seemed to possess an easy social accessibility. Bent over the table, she smiled upward at Peckham in friendly greeting, her half-discernible breasts almost like part of the buffet from which one was free to make his selections. She herself was heaping her plate with the chicken paprika that constituted the main dish. "My aunt threatens to disinherit me if I gain back the ten pounds I lost, but with a spread like this I'd say it was anybody's night to howl, wouldn't you?"

"Absolutely. I'm Earl Peckham."

"Binnie Aspenwall. Earl Peckham. I've heard about you."

"Not all bad, I hope." He forgave himself the inanity on the ground that there were few, if any, noninsipid responses to a conversational ploy like that. Aunt. Disinherit. Aspenwall. Then this was the niece of Mrs. DelBelly's, this mid-twenties nymph with the family eyes of Vermont-maple-syrup brown with whom he was in spirit already sporting under a needle spray in the inaugural frolic he had promised himself. He soaped her smoothly sculptured shoulders, the breasts pouting under his touch as his palms traveled southward, ever more tenderly southward, across the firm dimpled belly toward the coral flanges of ah hoo boy. He was on fire, quenchless under the foaming waterfall . . .

"I'm going to pig out on these string beans with water chestnuts too."

"I see there are no place cards or anything," Peckham said as they edged down toward the salad and the wine at the end of the buffet. "Are you committed to a table with anybody or anything or . . ."

"Or can you pick me up? Sure."

At length they stood together with a plate in one hand and wine in the other, surveying the busy scene. She spotted an unoccupied table for two, jerked her head toward it, and hurried over to preempt it.

A cloud or two hung over this glorious good fortune, which Peckham was anxious to disperse as soon as possible.

"It's probably your aunt who may have mentioned running across me at Dappled Shade, but I'm there convalescing from hepatitis, not because I put firecrackers in people's mailboxes or eat pie crust-first. That's why this wine I took is a second glass for you." He hoped that would be a sufficient cue for Binnie to amplify on what she had "heard" about him, so he wouldn't have to fish anymore. It was.

"She says you work your mouth pretty good." Peckham was relieved to sense that the girl was laughing at the expression rather than at him. "So I expect to hear some dazzling conversation."

"I do like beautiful words. Like Aspenwall. Are there just scads of you around?"

"No, I'm the last of the line. That's what I was joking about a minute ago anent the overeating and Aunt Nelly's disapproval. Did I use that word right—*anent?* I've always wanted to use it."

"Quite right. It's principally Scottish and regional English, though, of course, obsolete. But that you knew."

"Wow, I'm getting impressed with myself. It's one of those archaic words you use in fun, like . . . Help me."

"Yclept. You're yclept Binnie Aspenwall. That's old— no, wait a minute. That's Middle English."

"Jesus. If my aunt could hear me now she *would* disinherit me. You're a writer."

Everything she had said and done so far, in no more than five minutes' time, had painted the portrait of an inveterate flirt. The flip jokes about disinheritance only served to augment her physical lusciousness with the reminder that she was in addition an heiress. Did the fact imply that *all* the money represented here would pass to her and whomever she eventually married? As far back as the buffet table Peckham had noted that the left hand was barren of any rings. Was she eligible? Was he? He moved swiftly to offset any havoc Mrs. DelBelly might potentially have wrought his cause by relating the moonlight incident and the demoralizing chase scene that had followed.

"I should forewarn you that I'm shameless in my researches into human behavior, simply to get authenticity into what I write. I was stuck in a new novel at a point exactly reproduced by a situation with your aunt the other day, and so to provoke her into the, well, feminine reaction I wanted to describe, I deliberately . . ." He unfolded the same rigmarole he had with the aunt, in hopes that it would save his bacon here. This girl had taken him by storm, with all visible defects taken into account. She had a steady rippling speech with an undercurrent of amusement breaking out at intervals into open and frank laughter, though seldom of a malicious kind. And did they dry one another down, those shower-taking lovers? Was that part of the ritual, caressively blotting one another with those enormous terry-cloth towels in which one saw them making their way back to bed in the movies? "So I may say something deliberately to shock you."

"O.K. Cheers. Sorry I have to drink alone, but here's to your liver." She took a generous gulp, with an odd sidelong look somewhere, at the same time slightly lowering her head, as though worried that she might be observed. She licked her lips and set the glass down. "So shoot. Say something to shock me."

"Not now. That's part of the game. To take you unawares."

"Please do." This in a tone of mock coquettishness that was itself the coquettishness it mocked. How could he not hope a conquest lay within his grasp?

"How long does it take you to write a book?"

"Varies. Writing a book is like a long bout of illness," he said, seeing little call to give his source for the remark to one who could scarely have read Orwell. "So you're the last of the line. Too bad, if the tree was anything like the sprig I'm looking at."

"There was just Daddy as Aunt Nell's sole brother, and my mother, who died even before he did. Uncle Frank himself left no known heirs. My aunt says you have loads of personality."

"What's so funny about that?"

"The expression. I'd never heard it before, so I figured

it was something from the horse-and-buggy days. Have
you?"

"Noo. Well, come to think of it, I did hear my grandfather use it."

"So you'd as soon come down with hepatitis as find
yourself with book again. Are you with book now?"

"It could be."

"Are we going back for seconds?"

"Let's not and say we did. Now *there's* a golden oldie.
Goes with 'twenty-three skidoo' and 'I love my wife but
oh, you kid.' Have you ever taken a shower with anybody?"

"Good God, why do you ask that?"

"I warned you it would come unawares. You see, I have
these two characters," Peckham improvised, "reminiscing
club-men actually, gazing into the fire as they remember
former loves and all that sort of thing, and they fall into
an argument about how standard a part of lovemaking
romps that is. Do you think couples do it a lot, Binnie?"

"Well, it's academic with me. I rarely take showers. I
much prefer a bath. Love to lie there and *soak.*"

"Well, then soak together. In the tub. It's the same
thing. Have you ever done that? You have a right to a
lawyer."

"Yech! Puddle around in somebody else's suds?"

So she was a *yecher* then, given to that current little
ejaculation which made its users themselves momentarily
deserve it. She might have an uphill battle for his affec-
tions at that, even allowing for his present collapse in
helpless infatuation at her feet. It was a stirring dilemma,
however grueling. With the aunt, it would mean settle-

64

ment for an unbedeviled but no doubt platonic union;
with this pretty, the smoke and flame of closer contact.
The latter might offer prime literary stuff had one the
tranquility of the other in which to compose it. But you
couldn't have it both ways, could you. He must stop shilly-
shallying and make up his mind which campaign to wage.
In a house this size (and they were soon to be given the
grand tour), bickering between two people could be conducted over an intercom. There probably already was one.
But when would the younger accede to the property? Maybe
not even in Peckham's lifetime, what with Mrs. DelBelly's
robust health. But the excitement of the chase—two
chases!—was keen. The question was how much wear and
tear on his nerves could he take? Especially in the even-
tuality of Option 1 making him this ravishing creature's
uncle.

"Oh, I don't know about that," he said, reverting to
the question of sloshing about *à deux*. "If you remember,
that's how Huxley's *Point Counter Point* ends. Burlap and
Beatrice splashing about in the bathtub together like children. That was Jesus Christ's point too. Unless we become
like little children we shall in no wise enter the kingdom
of heaven."

"Yeah, well, I guess I'm not the religious type." Binnie
set her fork down on a finally empty plate and looked
toward the buffet, where a contingent of early returnees
for seconds mingled with late stragglers on their firsts. "Am
I swelling visibly under those evil green eyes of yours?
Hey, when are you going to shoot me the shocker?"

"I just did."

"That's it? About the shower? Pretty tame by today's standards. You must be a gentleman."

"To my fingertips. But that's where it ends." He flirted his eyebrows suggestively in the manner of a thousand Groucho Marx impressionists. What fun he was having disintegrating! Maybe he was in at Dappled Shade for more than he suspected.

"Anyway, the answer would have to be no in my case. I've never taken a shower with a man, but a girl is always open to new experiences. I'd have to be sure the guy was freshly bathed."

"Oh, I'd be all of that, quite agree with you on that score." He was working his mouth pretty good. "Let's go back for a nickel's worth. As my grandfather used to say when asking for a spot more at the dinner table."

Her own nickel's worth was rather generous, and she ate it with as much gusto as she had the first helping. To say nothing of the extra glass of wine she picked up for herself. Peckham thought it would have seemed a bit gross to get her another from his own allotment, as though he were trying to ply her with liquor. She was well into her third when he said, as though what she was drinking had loosened *his* tongue, "Might I see you sometime?"

This time she laughed as if in response to some element of comedy in what Peckham had asked, of which he was himself unaware. She looked into her glass as she swirled the wine about in it, tipping a few drops onto the table. Apparently she couldn't hold her liquor, welcome enough for a short-order seduction but hardly desirable in a wife.

"That would be nice from my pint of, my point of view.

But you will have to clear it with my fiancé. You're looking at my finger again. No, he hasn't given me a ring yet. The engagement hasn't been consummated."

"I'm sorry. I hadn't realized. I mean it didn't seem as though you came with someone," Peckham stammered, his mouth drying and his tongue appearing clogged in some remnant of Dogwinkle's peanut butter.

"That's Dempster over there."

She directed his gaze to a thirtyish scowl several tables away, in the direction in which she had been worriedly glancing from her first glass. Deciding that the young man looked like a dempster slightly assuaged Peckham's humiliation. The dempster was a creature, created on the spot, with a square jaw quite unlike the tapering snout of his nearest and smallest relative, the hamster. But like the hamster he was a hoarder, collecting provisions—in this case money—in large cheek pouches for later leisurely consumption. The dark watchful eyes, momentarily darted in their direction with a clear proprietorial jealousy, bespoke the fortune hunter. Well, it was what Miss Aspenwall deserved, if her ready self-advertisement as an heiress was as characteristic as seemed. They would have three handsome children, two cars and a harlequin Dane named either Hamlet or Ophelia, depending on the sex. If she and Dempster became his niece and nephew respectively, by virtue of Peckham's marriage to Mrs. DelBelly after all, a firm fiduciary hand would be required, trust funds already set up notwithstanding. For it was back on the front burner with Mrs. DelBelly.

"I do like you, Earl of Peckham, so maybe we can have

67

a foursome or something. If you haven't got a girl here, Dempster and I know several quite nice ones. I mean if you fancy being fixed up with blind dates."

"Let's get someone for Dempster instead," he cracked, and she like to split a gut. As they said back home where he came from. It certainly resolved the tension. How happily silly they were once again, as though the three glasses of wine Binnie consumed were flowing through both their veins. Her woozy gaiety was quite contagious. Mrs. DelBelly watched from the front burner. He caught sight of her out of the tail of his eye, sitting with Dr. Hushnecker at the table next to Dempster's. Yes, he was having fun disintegrating. He must do it oftener, though this lark was not without certain volatile impurities. He was cheating on Mrs. DelBelly at her own housewarming. Had he the makings of a bounder all along, never suspecting it for all his Svengalian strain? What a paradox he was, but then aren't we all. The dempster was taking all this in too, with the same watchfulness as the aunt's. Then, turning his attention back to Binnie, he found *her* taking him in as sharply as the other two. She regarded him with a thoughtful scrutiny.

"It's your eyes," she said. Her elbows on the table edge, she rested her chin on hands folded upside down. "Those— I hope you won't mind this—those little gooseberries seem to look right through one. I don't mean *see* through a girl, but *look* through her. As though with some . . . Oh, I shouldn't say it."

"Go ahead. Say it." He found himself tingling from the toes up. What man doesn't like being told by a woman that he's not to be trusted with women?

"Some hypnotic purpose."

"Please."

"It's true. Put you in mussy-messy clothes, instead of that freshly pressed tweed and tie that goes well with it, give you greasy stringy hair instead of neatly parted, and you'd be another Svengali. I say that because I just saw Barrymore in a revival of the movie, and the thought just happened to cross my mind. Probably also in part because of the bathtub business. Because there's a scene in the picture where Svengali, Barrymore, is in the tub and he looks up with the most crucified-Christ look. It's ham and it's funny but it's also memorable. Did you ever see the picture?"

"Oh sure. And if letting my hair get long and greasy and wearing baggy clothes would give me the same power over you he has over Trilby, why, I might just try it."

"Now you're poking fun at me."

If she only knew how wrong that was! His sharpest adolescent memory was of a date with a notoriously chaste girl in his father's car, and a lover's-lane petting session where the ravishing ninny had drawn back from his advances and said, "You hypmatize me. You could have your will of me, Earl, but I'm going to be strong and say no." And with that she had plucked his venturing hand from her mid-thigh. She'd carried this girlish dramatization to absurd lengths. One summer day, she agreed to "leave him go shopping with her" for a bathing suit, and having plumped for a blue one likely to meet with parental approval, had let him override her choice by taking the more revealing red he preferred, further evidence of a power over her verging on the diabolical. It was "best" that a vacation with her folks would remove her from his spell for a time. All that high-school foolishness came back to him now, with a rather more gratifying resonance than memory had hitherto yielded.

"Well, the Svengali or Rasputin stuff doesn't seem to be working, what with your response to my request for a simple conventional dinner date."

"I'll change the no to a maybe, maybe. Look, let's get dessert. I think Aunt Nell is chafing at the bit to get dinner over with and on to the grand tour, or everybody'll be here till all hours."

Trooping by the score through nearly a score of rooms took organization and command. At the head of the procession marched the hostess, looking with each step more like a Valkyrie guiding the deserving into Valhalla, together with her decorator, Tommy Heilbrunner, and Heilbrunner's wife. Tommy explained how the place had been done over, from new upholstery and draperies to more drastic alterations such as incidental carpentry and a "kitchen reconception." It was in one of the six or seven bedrooms upstairs that Peckham formally met the near-fiancé, if that was how to interpret Binnie's report that "the engagement hasn't been consummated." Leaving Peckham to wonder whether the joke had been conscious or unconscious. A dingbat might well lurk under the surface intelligence. She had been half in her cups when she'd said it, so maybe it too was half-conscious and half-unconscious. "I'd like you to meet Dempster Hyster. Dempster, this is Earl Peckham."

It was odd and no doubt more than a little perverse to go on mentally emphasizing his resemblance to a dempster, since it was his name that had created the creature he resembled. He had dark curly hair, large eyes nearly as black, the full cheeks in which food was hoarded by the species and a handshake that ground the bones in Peckham's fingers—warning of what he might do in the way of wringing an interloper's neck. It was then in the fifth of the bedrooms that Peckham got separated from the pair, apparently by some designing maneuver of Dempster's. Because Peckham next caught sight of them engaged in some kind of argument in a corner apart. He was obviously scolding her for her tipsy condition, in a way that suggested a standard lecture on her not realizing by now her poor tolerance for alcohol. "Should know better" was one whispered rebuke Peckham caught, and then something about "every Tom, Dick and Harry." Could Peckham be considered every Tom, Dick and Harry? He would hardly have suspected it and under another code of honor might have called the chap out at dawn for the slur. Binnie flounced smartly away and managed to lose herself in the thick of the crowd, which was now traipsing along into still another bedroom.

Why would a woman living alone want half a dozen or more bedrooms all furnished as for normal and regular usage? A young man with whom Peckham fell into conversation explained that Nelly loved to entertain a lot, three weekend couples being by no means unusual. That didn't sit well with Peckham, who liked being neither a guest nor a host. For himself, he picked a bedroom with

71

a fine view of the garden and a meadow beyond, and an anteroom that would serve admirably as a study. Mrs. DelBelly's own master bedroom was a bower of pink and blue, with a canopy bed all afluff with eiderdown so thick it looked as though it had been pumped up, and a chaise longue that was a model of luxury in its own right. The baths all had tubs alone, but these were equipped with sliding glass panels behind which were shower heads, leaving the question of tandem ablutions absolutely open to option. He suddenly wondered where Binnie lived. Might it be right here with her aunt? They were all making their way back downstairs toward the reconceived kitchen when he managed once more to sidle in next to her and ask the question that struck him as strange not to have occurred to him before.

"Where do you live, my dear?"

"Parkson," she said, naming a nearby residential hotel. The altercation seemed to have got her spirit up, to near the point of anger. "Look, I'll have dinner with you sometime. Why not? Just for the hell of it, you understand."

"Of course. Just for the plain unadulterated hell of it."

FOUR

They drove in Binnie's red Jaguar convertible to a small French restaurant two or three towns away, after meeting like conspirators at a crossroads half a mile from the main gate of Dappled Shade, to which Peckham walked after signing out and under pretense of going out for a stroll. He explained his absence from the sanitarium dinner table on the ground that he wasn't hungry. Selecting a dimly lit corner table on top of all this hugger-mugger made their little peccadillo, he told Binnie, resemble intrigue as the mist resembles the rain. "What, *what* a lip," she said. The allusion to Longfellow got them on the subject of poetry in general, and Binnie said her term paper for senior college English had been on Frost, which got Peckham on a short disquisition relating to Frost's use of inversion, something more or less lifted from his own classroom lectures.

"It's one way to get a poetic effect. I mean, 'I think I know whose woods these are' isn't poetry. 'Whose woods these are I think I know' is. 'There is something that doesn't love a wall' isn't poetry. 'Something there is that doesn't love a wall' makes it."

"You're a writer," Binnie told him for the second time. "Are you famous?"

"My name is a household word. Except in the average home, of course. Give us a kiss."

True, he could not love her half so much loved he not honor more. True, were they still in the close quarters of the car, or even seated at right angles to one another in this snug corner, he might have been regarded as asking for something quite intimate, or prolongable as such. But they were sitting across the table from one another, so that the need to rise from his chair to avail himself of her playfully pursed lips, holding his necktie to keep it from lolling into his plate of sweetbread or picking up a spot of butter, absolved him from having asked for anything more than a peck on the mouth. That given, no soul gazes followed, as though she might come out with a shopgirl's "Oh, Earl, what'll we do?" In fact she lowered her head and, hand to brow, began to shake with laughter.

"What, what?"

"I'm sorry. I was just thinking of something Aunt Nelly said. 'He ought to have his marbles examined.' I'm sorry. It's the way she talks, you know. Getting expressions wrong."

"I know that. But of whom was she speaking? That ought to have his marbles examined."

"You."

"I see." He finished off a gobbet of sweetbread in silence. Then he asked, "And did you correct her?"

"Well, no, I wasn't going to say, 'No, Aunt Nelly,' the expression is "He doesn't have all his marbles".' Or 'Do you think he has all his marbles?' That would have been rude, wouldn't it?"

"Of course. That's not what I meant. I meant, did you give her an argument? Dispute what she'd said."

"Oh, for Christ's sake, Earl, of course I pooh-poohed her."

"Briskly? Tepidly? Pooh-poohing can be subject to a wide spectrum of interpretations."

"Spectrum schmectrum. Of course I told her the whole thing was too silly for words. As this argument is. And in the middle of this divine meal. How are your sweetbreads? This veal is wonderful. Might I have another glass of wine?"

"You've had one large one, after a martini. Well, I suppose it's O.K., with me driving. But then I'll have to walk all the way back from your apartment. That's a good two miles. I suppose I should have my marbles examined at that. Well, I'll be going to the right place."

"I like that domineering way you have of letting a girl have her own way. No, not domineering, I shouldn't say that. Dominating is more like it, because you don't really try. It's just your masterful way, of being in charge. You're a gem, Earlie. And I see now it's the way you have of *narrowing* your eyes that does it. You seem to see right into a person."

"We're not going to have that Svengali business again, I hope," he objected halfheartedly. When she did not immediately respond, being more attentive to the waiter's fetching her fresh glass of wine, he pursued the matter himself. "If I'm so dominating, how does that square with letting you have your own way?"

"Well, that's just it. *You* decide when to yield and when to put your foot down. But you're always in charge. Even with yourself. Can't you have just one teeny glass? Don't you want to live the good life?"

"It depends on the liver. Believe me, August fifteenth is circled on my calendar as a red-letter day. That's when the doc said."

He waited till the waiter had brought her wine and left, before asking the question on his mind.

"What was the occasion for your aunt's remark? What prompted her?"

"I told her you asked me for a date."

"And did you tell her I hung off when I learned you had a steady? Christ, has that word crossed my lips?"

"Actually that didn't come into it, I mean it never had a chance. Because I said no. That was all she wanted to know. That I'm not playing around."

"Well, that little omission of yours leaves me pretty much in her bad books. Rather out of pocket, morally, wouldn't you say? To continue this quite justified cross-examination, did you tell her you finally agreed?"

"Good God no. She'd have fallen through the ceiling, another expression she gets wrong. She'd consider that being unfaithful to Dempster."

The accumulating casuistry of all this seemed to Peckham like a clump of barbed wire into which his foot became all the more hopelessly entangled with every effort to shake free of it. The struggle continued even after dinner when she directed him up a series of winding near-country roads for an hour's ramble during which nothing would do but that they ride with the top down, to cool off. What was needed was a little warming up. For the spirit between them had quite cooled with the threat of a set-to at the table. Peckham tried to restore their earlier mood with a few reminiscences of his own about her aunt's garbled expressions, trusting that the affectionate amusement with which he shared them offset the fact that he was offering her up as sacrificial lamb in an attempt to make hay with a niece of whose present shenanigans she would have heartily disapproved.

"She thinks it's the old lady in Peoria and will it play in Dubuque." My God, what was happening to him? That was Dogwinkle who got the two screwed around. Oh, well, it made no difference. It sounded like her and might just very well have been true to the facts. And indeed there wasn't a spark of malice in his recollections, but they bolstered his wavering resolve that, yes, the aunt must be relegated once and for all to the back burner, if not removed from the stove altogether.

He turned to steal a glance at Binnie. She was leaning with her head back, eyes closed, blond hair blowing in the wind, the full scarlet lips slightly parted in pleasure. He went ill with desire. But there was still the barbed-wire tangle of casuistry to get himself honorably out of. Sexual emancipation was all very well until you got into bed. Then the question of moral obligations began to gnaw you.

"Look, you'll remember that I didn't press you for this date after I learned you and Dempster were a thing. We're only out together now because you picked up on it later, after some sort of tiff." Picking up on this or that was apparently a term used by the young.

"Do you want to sleep with me?"

"You said your engagement hadn't been consummated, thereby ushering in a new era you might say—"

She slid erect with a burst of laughter, then swung around to face him, her legs drawn up on the leather seat.

"Did I say that?"

"If you don't remember, then it's because you were in your cups at the time or you are now. Incidentally, it doesn't seem to take many cups with you. You can't hold your liquor, toots. But to get back to your question. I'm not a mouse, but I'm not a rat either. I'd never try to horn in on a betrothal. That would be nastier than being a housewrecker."

"I know."

She lapsed back into the previous sober mood, which quickly became a somber one. She directed him through a series of turns that brought them back to her place. He garaged the car for her, kissed her in the lobby outside her elevator door, promised to phone her, and said good night as lyrically as possible with both the elevator operator and the desk clerk looking on. He went out the front door with head averted until he could wipe the lipstick from his mouth in the street. The two-mile walk back to Dappled Shade, originally rather dreaded, turned out to offer a welcome opportunity to cool off and sort out his thoughts.

Not that the last was by any means conclusive. For two days he stewed in a caldron of pros and cons, passions and anxieties, crescendoes and diminuendoes, urges and counterurges, delights and doubts, impulses to phone and admonitions not to, hopes that Binnie herself might call mingled with fears that she would. At last she did, suggesting they meet for a drink. She would pick him up at the same place around four-thirty. That was all it was, a drink at a tavern she fancied, meaning another virgin Mary for him, and after the same moral rehash as had marked their first date, she dropped him off where she had picked him up. Frustration if anything intensified his moral turmoil.

The crisis was blessedly resolved by others.

Dr. Hushnecker fingered a paper knife suitable for slitting either one's morning correspondence or, so it occurred to Peckham watching across the desk, an adversary's throat. As a sort of nervous compromise, he slipped it in and out between the blotter on his desk and the pad into which the blotter fitted at the four corners. It was notable how we operated on fours, Peckham mused as he awaited some word from Hushnecker, who had the air of a principal who had called a pupil in for some kind of disciplinary action. We sat on four-legged chairs in rooms with four walls, talked of the four winds of an in fact circular sky, must have exactly four Gospels, consigning all the rest written to the limbo of apocrypha. There were four freedoms, four dimensions and even four horsemen. We had ourselves once been quadrupeds, and still were on occasion, such as Peckham's morning hunt for a fifty-cent piece that had rolled under his bed, following a rough night at Manderley. A fruitless search for shower stalls there had supplied the scenario for his latest "frustration dream," with Mrs. DelBelly grumbling impatiently in his wake in a bathrobe, towel over her shoulder. The doctor finally settled on the length to which the knife blade was to be inserted under the blotter, as though symbolically deciding on the exact degree of familiarity with which this session was to be conducted. At last he said:

"Would you say you had all your marbles?"

"That's for me to know and you to find out. Ah hoo boy," Peckham secretly thought to himself, that's one for old Gramps and his generation all right, and for Binnie's and my scrapbook of vintage snaperoos, already bidding fair to be "our" shtick. For audible purposes he amended the rejoinder to, "Wouldn't that be rather for you to say?" Emphasizing the tinge of irony by squinching his face up in the manner of Clark Gable, while thus at the same time retaining the sense of amenities. He might also have said, "Go peddle your papers" or "Go home and tell your mother she wants you." It was obvious from the doctor's layman's language that the session had been inspired by Mrs. DelBelly, even granted his professed avoidance of psychiatric jargon wherever possible. It was obvious this was a cat-and-mouse, with no clear certainty as to which was which.

"I'll come right to the point. Mrs. DelBelly is curious."

Peckham could be forgiven the tremor of pleasure he felt at this. Did it mean that, after all, she took at face value his halting efforts as a suitor and did not dismiss them out of hand? At least she knew he was alive (or speaking clinically as of the moment, half-alive).

The doctor tilted back in his swivel chair far enough to cross his legs and drew a long breath.

"Courtship, or coming on to someone, as the young people say today, is a very tricky business, of which the aggressor is often morally unaware, breeding both deceptions and confidences. We talked quite frankly about you the other evening, and it's obvious she likes you, however much an oddball she considers you. Hence the question. I had to tell her candidly when it was posed to me that I know little more about you than she does, since our interviews have consisted principally in my advising you about the hepatitis you enrolled here for a rest from. So up to now I've played merely the M.D., as has Dr. Auslese, with whom I had a brief chat awhile ago about the larger aspect."

"About my marbles."

"Yes, if you want to put it that way. He leans more to the Viennese terminology," Dr. Hushnecker added with a smile, "while I'm more your, well, meat and potatoes. Would you say you had them?"

"Meat and potatoes?"

"No, no, marbles."

"If I don't who does?"

"Do you mean who has any missing marbles of yours, or who among us has all of his own?"

"That depends on who's on first. Or as our dear, dear Mrs. DelBelly puts it, who's up first? Which is of course just as funny. If not funnier."

"This is not a funny farm. You have a very charming schoolboy way of getting the teacher off on a tangent, so he must rap a few knuckles and get us back to the geography lesson. We were talking about courtship, and the jump back from this isn't far. Because we know damn well that patients often try to con us the way we do each other in courtship, putting our best foot forward, snowing one another till we're married and even long into that. Marriages often become a shambles because the parties had used courtship to snow each other. In a word, you never know whether the melon is any good till you get it home and cut it open."

"I assure you I have never practiced any kind of deception with Nelly DelBelly. I'm a quartered melon for her or anybody to see, or taste."

The doctor looked quizzically across the desk, drawing the paper knife out from under the blotter like a sword from its sheath.

"We don't seem to be connecting here. When I speak of courtship *now* I have in mind Mrs. DelBelly and *me*. My God, you mean you didn't know—?"

"My God, you mean you and—?" Largely feigned surprise, of course.

"Of course. I thought you realized that and surmised that I was switching now to her and me as an item, as they say today. We're as good as engaged."

"Has the engagement been consummated?"

It had just popped out, as Hushnecker threatened to pop out of his chair—that is, use it as a catapult to hurl himself across the desktop at Peckham, having in midflight firmly grasped the paper knife for use as a dagger.

"I meant have you given her a ring, of course," Peckham stammered.

"I see," Hushnecker said, settling back again. "Not quite yet."

"May I offer you my congratulations."

"Thank you."

"Then why, may I ask, is she casing me? Marbles-wise and so on."

"Because of your interest in her niece. She spotted its inception the other night at the housewarming, where, I might add, it was unmistakable to everyone, not excluding Dempster Hyster, *her* intended. And we all know you've been out with her since."

"With Sam Spade looking for her?"

"What?"

"Nothing."

"Young Binnie seems to like you—as indeed do we all. As they must have liked Dylan Thomas when he cut *his* swath down the eastern seaboard." Peckham was permitted a brief simper, downward glancing, before the doctor continued. "Incidentally, you might remember what happened to *his* liver. I'm sure you'll be a little more prudent. Where were we? Binnie Aspenwall, yes. If her interest in you were allowed to become serious, it could mean rough water with *that* engagement. And you may be sure Mrs. DelBelly has a mother-hen proprietorial interest in it, apart from how far into the next county Dempster would knock you. He pumps iron at the Y."

His elbows on the arms of his chair, Peckham folded his hands with his forefingers pressed in a triangle to pursed lips, as he had seen colleagues do during more vapid moments of faculty conferences, and nodded thoughtfully. His aim was to breathe an air of personal probity while at the same time savoring what could be humanly taken as a testimonial to one's success with women. The latter often as not left a man free to extract some perverse egotistical satisfaction from the charge that he was a "rotter." He forgave himself for savoring the implication that he had made, at forty-two, early headway with a young woman little more than half that age.

"Then all in all it's best for everyone that you're going on this whirlwind autographing tour. How are the sales of your book?"

"Astounding."

"Good. Glad to hear it. Can we shake hands on this, gentleman to gentleman, as well as two men of the world?"

"I'll be out of town by sunset."

The promise to do so became very nearly literal as well as figurative.

The next afternoon as he was sunning himself in one of the Adirondack chairs he saw a figure cross the lawn toward him with tread purposeful. He stood squarely before Peckham, looking more than ever like a dempster, whether plying the treadmill or snuffling his pellet food. He declined the chair to which Peckham waved him, preferring to remain on his feet while he said what he had to say. Peckham tilted his Panama hat upward off his brow, the better to see him.

"I think you've seen Bin often enough, and in an apparently serious enough sense, for one to reasonably ask what your intentions are."

"I intend to sweep her off to Carthage and Cathay, to Cotopaxi and to Ind, and thence along the golden road to Samarkand."

"They're right. You do work your mouth pretty good."

Jesus! How these expressions got around here, in this tight little circle.

"Why don't you take this up with Bin herself?" Peckham said. "She's the one to whom this is the more germane."

"Germane schmermane."

Not again!

"One might be forgiven for wondering what exactly your prospects are. Whether you're capable of supporting her in the style to which she's been accustomed." The clichés rained so profusely that Peckham found himself saying in sheer self-defense, "Material possessions aren't everything. It's what a person is inside," he added, with a spasm of revulsion.

"For example, it's reasonable to ask how well you sell. I'm in the advertising business, and I happen to know what the average novel does."

"My books do well enough. They're not your average novel."

Dempster grunted. "Well, with my connections I can find out soon enough from your publisher."

"No!"

The reply was torn from him like a cry of pain. The thought that Binnie Aspenwall, to say nothing of all the rest, would learn that *Sorry Scheme* had sold a total of three copies was unendurable.

He rose to his feet, adjusting the Panama, which nearly fell off his head in the abrupt movement. In fact, his reflexes fairly recalled W. C. Field's perpetual business with his headgear.

"Forget it. Your snorting threats and glowering expressions are quite absurdly unnecessary. I'm leaving here in a day or two and that will be that, the end of this entirely uncalled-for brouhaha. And neither you, Binnie nor Nell DelBelly will ever see me again." How wrong he was there! But that was not the point, for the moment. The point was that he turned and marched toward the house, stung to the quick by the shame of having committed, as a parting shot, the awful barbarism of a three-pronged neither-nor. He needed a rest, after this place.

FIVE

The two bookstores that had ordered copies of *Sorry Scheme* (other than the one here in Westchester) lay deep in our great American heartland, showing there was hope for the country, if not exactly a burning hunger for subtle literature. One was in Cedar Rapids, Iowa, a state with a very high literacy rate, Peckham had heard, second in the country after New York, he had been told; the other in Omaha. It had taken some telephoning to extract their identities from sighing functionaries on the other end of the line at his publisher's billing department, but extract them he had, and here he was on his way to a hinterland far more deserving of respect than the supposedly educated East, if you asked Peckham.

He wasn't making this trip solely to visit the stores in question, though that curiosity was natural, given the facts; it was a sort of occasion for the cross-country ramble he had always found the ideal holiday for him. The first leg of his journey was a bus trip to Cleveland where both he and his Chevrolet Citation had conked out a few months previous, coming *East*. The car's transmission had collapsed just as Peckham's hepatitis broke out. A doctor taken potluck from the yellow pages had advised him to hospitalize himself as soon as possible, and preferring to do that in New York, where he lived, he left the Chevy for a transmission overhaul and wobbled, sweating profusely, onto the first plane he could get for home. He would now recover the car where it had lain in dead storage ever since and continue the westward push from there. Unbeknownst to Peckham, the copy he had signed in the Westchester shop had already been returned, exposing rotten Dogwinkle's radical misinformation about the unreturnability of books so disfigured, and so in that general regard this trip could turn out to be a wild-goose chase. Its value was of the other, restorative kind, and as he lolled back in his bus seat he tried not to think of the money end of it. Some bills were ripening steadily on his Village desk back home, but they were not from merchants with whom he was in particularly bad odor as a deadbeat, so a period of grace could be taken for granted there.

He had had a bad night, not for want of sleep, but owing to the continuing drain of his dreams. Things were going poorly at Manderley, what with the struggle to cram Mrs. DelBelly alone into the single shower stall finally discovered there in a remote corner of the estate and close the door behind her, so that he and Binnie could watch her through the translucent door. And so it continued to go, o'nights. Now Peckham tried to strike up a conversation with the first of his bus mates, a brick-red man who got on at Newark and sat tensely upright with his hands on his kneecaps, as though nursing them along after fractures inflicted for payment arrears by loan-shark goons. Once they were bowling through open country the man seemed to relax a little, at least to the extent of sharing some testy opinions.

"Glad to be free of the billboards I just been through on my connecting trip. Blight on the frigging landscape. Toothpaste, soft drinks, frigging breakfast foods. Spoiling what's left of the frigging country."

"Frigging country is good," Peckham agreed. He saw a chance to practice his newly found gift for maxims of unconscionable length and opacity. His improvisations had become increasingly more labyrinthine, not uniformly enthralling to his hearers except for intellectual soulmates capable of appreciating contents idiotic by design and thus intended in a surrealist-dadaist vein to travesty folk pith, especially of the imported kind. Television was forging a nation of clods turning, when they read at all, to increasingly imbecile bestseller lists. He had actually seen a man enter a store armed with such a list, clipped from the *Times* book section, and use it to buy a number of titles for his "summer reading." It had been the Doubleday shop where Mrs. DelBelly had seen Tennessee Williams enthroned at the autographing table, on her way downcellar to purchase a murder mystery. "I'm just your average reader," she had said, rather giving herself airs, it seemed to Peckham now in retrospect. He had been wise to dump her.

"The ancient Persians had a saying," he chatted to the brick-red passenger. "A man unable to appreciate a landscape qua landscape, randomly composed to delight the eye and soothe the spirit, however seemingly assembled

from fortuitous elements both geological and botanical—
and in fact even if consciously so apprehended by one
skeptical of teleological principles at work anywhere in
the cosmos—such a man might be regarded by his fellows
as esthetically handicapped, just as we categorize parallel
deficiencies with the terms physically or morally handicapped. In that regard permit me—"

"Look, Mac, I'm not in no mood to permit nothing. I
happen to suffer from motion sickness, as a child I got
dizzy just sitting on a porch glider, but I have to go on to
Bethlehem, nauseous or not. I don't want to hear about
no ancient Persians of old, especially in sentences that
make me feel like I'm going around on a merry-go-round.
I'm a poor traveler, and that saying drug in the middle,
you ask me. I'm this far from woofing my breakfast as it
is, O.K.?"

"Certainly, my good fellow, anything you say. I was
only offering a thought instigated by your own well-taken
observation about the frigging environment."

"So if you don't want some used waffles in your lap."

"Hardly an upshot to be wished."

"You got it right with the upshot. I . . . in fact . . . feel
as though . . ."

"Easy on, old chap. Just relax. Journeys get to be boring
without passing the time in conversation. I was only trying
to chew the fat . . . "

"That does it. Driver!"

Like an ocean-goer heading for the ship's rail on a companion's imprudent allusion to prune whip or Hungarian
goulash, the passenger (now as much chartreuse green as

brick red) bolted to the front of the bus, where the driver instantly divined the problem, probably from long experiences with eliminative crises of all kinds, and screeching to a halt, simultaneously opened the door. The man rushed through it just in time to leave beside the road a volcanic eruption that to have been the recipient of which, lapwise, would have made the trip memorable indeed. He felt visibly relieved when he returned, and smiled apologetically as he resumed his seat beside Peckham, who told him to think nothing of it. They rolled along in relative silence, broken only by desultory remarks about other frigging things worthy of disapproval along the way, both finally adjusting their seats to lounge position and dozing off. There are few things more lulling than the drone of a motor.

That of his own finally recovered car threatened to make Peckham nod off behind the wheel more than once, so that on his way across Ohio he stopped in at an auto-parts store to buy something which he had heard called a Sleeper Beeper, a small battery-operated gadget that fit comfortably behind the ear and roused you with a piercing wail if your head so much as nodded. He sometimes settled for seedy-looking motels for the night rather than push on to cities offering the possibility of more savory accommodations. For he occasionally wandered off his established route up a beckoning byroad, meandering extemporaneously back to it again down some equally seductive course, thus to foster the pleasant sense of vagabondage. And he broke every day's portion of his odyssey to pause in whatever town likewise took his fancy. There was none so dreary, so tiny, so hamletesque and drowned in anonymity that, if traversed for half an hour's stroll, did not yield some aura worth the noting, beat with some unique pulse worth the catching. Of course within every such relish of appreciation lurked the rather guilt-ridden sense of freedom to push on: one was not stuck here, thank God. So ran the often wincing thought, not unstreaked with pity for those who might secretly themselves feel the burden of mortal confinement. Peckham tried to ignore that always ignoble taint and savor the houses and shops within which any such might live and labor out their days here in the middle of nowhere, their sorrow unsuspected. He loved the shaded commons and the everlasting Main Streets for the special flavor they collectively possessed and, possessing, gave off; their mystic appeal to private memories of which one has lost the thread, the muffled measure of bittersweet music echoing deep within the soul of the briefly tarrying wayfarer, sounding its last ephemeral note as he hurries away with the ever-aching human thought, "I shall not pass this way again." These sensations were as much invitations to melancholy as ingredients in an exquisite pleasure, and he had them merely driving through a village or city as well as stopping to saunter.

The additional poetry of Cedar Rapids lay in its containing somewhere in its nocturnal heart, for he arrived at nightfall, the single copy of *Sorry Scheme* that had found its way to Iowa. He knew the name of the shop, Barclay's Book Nook. Did the forlorn volume still lurk on a shelf or table there, wedged in among a thousand unknown fellows, or had it been bought and was it now reposing on a shelf or table in somebody's house? If the latter, whose? He would never know, except that it had blessedly found its way into the human stream. This admittedly irrational yet furiously itching curiosity would have to be satisfied by the Book Nook, not a very auspicious name, given the assumption of discerning selection.

Inquiries at his hotel supplied easy directions to its location, around the corner and a few blocks down, and he made for it the next morning after breakfast in the coffee shop. He took it in from across the street for a few minutes. It lived up, or down, to its name all right, taking up no more than twenty feet in the ground corner of a new-looking twenty-story office building. Probably one of those holes-in-the-wall one hears of obstinate old-timers refusing to yield to the march of crass real estate developers. The door looked barely wide enough to walk through, and both it and the narrow window were trimmed in flaking pink paint that by contrast with the building's chrome and glass sustained the fancy of a holdout valorously maintaining standards. One saw an aproned old lady in a rocker with a shotgun across her lap, protecting her own little scrap of property against rapacious promoters, now gone to her reward, leaving as her monument this little shop doughtily out of key with the gimcrackery heaved up all around it— a timeless rebuke. Now a thin middle-aged man with a scallion fringe of beard was crawling around in the window constructing an exhibition devoted to a single volume— "unidisplay" was the detested word Peckham heard for them in New York—and when Peckham made out the name of the novel, his own carefully erected theory about owners striking a blow for Taste collapsed in a heap. It was *Break Slowly, Dawn* by that Poppy McCloud whom Peckham had told their common publisher he was heartily unable to read. Anger revived his flagging nerve, and he strode across the street and into the store, a bell tinkling overhead.

The man, who on closer range looked like someone young who looked old for his age, turned on all fours and smiled from the window. He wore a blue neckband shirt, without the collar, blue jeans and soiled sneakers.

"Morning. I'll be right out."

"Don't hurry. Just browsing."

"Swell. Go right ahead."

Peckham was glad to see the man return to his task, which enabled him to wander the more freely about the shop in the search for *Sorry Scheme*. There were shelves along one wall, and two tables, one devoted to fiction, the other nonfiction. The former seemed crammed with novels of which there were only solitary copies wedged in tightly among each other, momentarily reviving the principle of meticulous selection on the part of the proprietor, with quality the object. Then why the mass emphasis on the No. 1 Bestseller in the window?

"I see you're going all-out for that piece of schnitzel."

"We have to do that nowadays to keep our heads above water." The chap made a cognoscente face, to indicate total rapport with Peckham as comember. "It's the bestsellers that enable stores to stay in business, as well as the very publishers themselves, more's the pity. At least we haven't had to put in gifts, bric-a-brac and greeting cards. Looking for anything in particular?"

"Not especially. Do you have *The Sorry Scheme of Things Entire?*"

"I believe . . ."

"Ah, here it is." The squiggle of red and green on the spine of the jacket leapt triumphantly up at him.

"I thought we had one copy left."

What a deft liar he is, Peckham thought, not without gratitude. One copy left, as though out of a stock of fifty that had melted like snow on the desert's dusty face. He drew it out forcibly and riffled through it like a bona fide browser. Leaving it faceup on the table, he edged his way around to the other side, winding up among the nonfiction just as the other set the last copy at the tip of the pyramid he had constructed and with a "There" sprang out of the window and down to the floor.

"Even with your rationalization about bestsellers buttering the old bread, that's quite a pile."

"Oh, she's coming through on an autographing barnstorm day after tomorrow and so we have to lay it on. She'll be on the local radio and get interviewed by the papers and so forth and so on. Big deal."

"Well, I'll be gone by then," Peckham said, and turned to the wall. The shelves there, labeled "Literature," contained standard authors, Modern Library editions and the like. The store's more or less permanent stock. The clerk, or proprietor, had been busying himself with something at the cash register counter, and when Peckham turned around he saw *Sorry Scheme* wasn't there where he had left it. It had been wrapped in violet paper and tied with a gilt string.

"That'll be thirteen-fifty."

"What?"

"The book you wanted."

"I didn't mean I—That is—The fact is, I'm the author."

"Ah ha! You're Earl Pelham. Well, I've been dying to meet you, and now I'm dead. Absolutely defunct." He extended his hand for a hearty shake. "We always like to have authors drop in. Seems to make it all worthwhile. Then of course you don't mean to buy it." He unwrapped it with an apologetic laugh.

"I'll be glad to autograph it."

"Super. Here's a pen. No, use this one. The blue ink is so much more attractive. Well, well. Earl Pelham in the flesh." He watched as Peckham scribbled his name on the flyleaf. "Now I'll put it in the window," he said, and again on all fours, crept carefully around his pyramid looking for a place to set it that would not leave it too dwarfed or obscured for the casual window-shopper. "Where are you stopping in our fair city?"

"The Winslow."

Peckham bought a book anyway, a volume almost picked at random that turned out to be something on occult phenomena, and as he passed the window on his way back up the street he glanced sidewise through the glass and caught a glimpse of his own work propped up behind it, open to the inscribed flyleaf. "One down and one to go," he thought, adding aloud if under his breath, "Ah hoo boy."

After a heavy lunch, he stretched out on his hotel-room bed and dipped into *More Things in Heaven and Earth*,

Horatio, reading half a chapter on telekinesis before dropping off. By chance, an apparently accredited case of it had recently cropped up in the news. A Des Moines man had been seen on television to make a gate swing open, sink a five-foot putt, and cause a maple sapling to bend in windless air, simply by staring hard at these objects and *willing* the desired result. The same psychic gift had been featured in a movie called *Carrie*, with Sissy Spacek overturning cars and directing carving knives at a vindictive mother in the same fashion. Peckham (Pelham indeed!), Peckham would pass through Des Moines and it might be worth hiring the man, for a fee, to topple the stack of *Break Slowly, Dawn* by similarly willing their collapse through the plate-glass window of the Book Nook, for a gathered audience of onlookers recruited for the event. Or better yet, at the Fifth Avenue B. Dalton, for one of their eternal blockbuster unidisplays, giving to him who hath and taking away from him who hath not even that which he hath. His last thought as he dozed away for his nap was how grotesque it was that he and Poppy McCloud had the same publisher. It was as grotesque as the fact that Chihuahuas and Saint Bernards were members of the same species.

He was awakened by the phone screaming in his ear.

"Mr. Pelham?"

"No, Peckham." Christ, he hoped it wasn't the character in the Book Nook, asking to join him in a drink.

"Yes. The writer. I'm on the local *Sentinel*, and Jack Hammond at the bookstore just called to tell me you were in town, and I was wondering if I might interview you. I could come to your room any time that's convenient, though I'd like to make it in twenty minutes or half an hour, so I can squeeze it into tomorrow morning's edition. Like to pop our VIPs right in, you know."

"All right," Peckham agreed in his stupor.

"Cool. My name is Looply. See you in a half then."

Looply was a brisk-mannered sorrel with an orange mustache which he kept combing with his lower teeth, or seemed to from his habit of so biting his upper lip with them. Peckham's heart sank at the sight of the tape recorder he was clutching in one hand. A cursed device to fix in permanent form the inanities into which one was forced by inane questions. Looply lost no time in asking them.

"Glad to see you in our fair city," be began heartily.

"It's more than fair. It's terrific," Peckham said, in an attempt to get off on the right foot, knowing from even scant past experience that it would soon be in his mouth.

"Well, thank you. Our readers will be glad to learn that's your opinion, Mr. Pelham. Where do you live in real life?"

"Peckham. New York."

"I know this is a question writers hate, but they're always asked it, owing to our, uh, awe with creative accomplishments of which we ourselves are not equal. Where do you get your ideas?"

Peckham didn't actually mind the question, having ready a reply with which Einstein himself dealt with the absurdity. "Well, actually, I've only had one or two ideas." Remorseful for the fool he was making of Looply, or rather for the fool he was letting Looply make of himself, he hastened to add, "As Einstein answered when asked that question. And by the way, my name is Peckham, Earl Peckham, and I live in the West Village, Greenwich Village, you understand, and the novel I'm making this whirlwind autographing tour of . . ." He paused to mend his unraveling syntax for the implacable recorder. "My book is entitled *The Sorry Scheme of Things Entire*. Title is from Omar."

"Omar . . .?"

"Khayyám," Peckham said, wondering how *that* would come out in print. "You know, the *Rubáiyát*." Or *that*.

Looply thought a moment, consulting a sheet of paper on which were apparently scribbled a list of questions to ask. Then he said, "Who would you say your major influences are?"

"Debussy and Ravel."

The other's expression indicated that he realized his leg was being pulled and that he was slightly hurt by it, as though he were being made a monkey of. But this time Peckham's instant penitence was as instantly followed by the question "Why not?" Personal temperaments do cross artistic boundaries, and who was to say the sense of verbal nuance to be found in the sentences he put down on a page had not their counterparts in the subtle, delicately dissonant harmonics that made these two composers his absolute favorites. He therefore picked up seriously on what had been uttered in jest.

"They are, to me, kindred spirits—not of course that I would presume to put myself in their class any more than I would that of Fitzgerald or Max Beerbohm, had I said *they* were my chief influences, which in a comparable sense they are. Why should what you listen to influence you any less than what you read? You see?"

"Oh, *I* see."

"Well, then, so there you are," Peckham answered, as though he were a character in a Henry James novel.

The next question made Peckham half jump out of his chair, as though an electric charge had unexpectedly reached an angry nerve.

"What do you think of Poppy McCloud?"

"Why?" he stalled, torn between the demands of courtesy and those of honesty. He felt like a rapidly unraveling rope in a tug-of-war between the two. God alone knew what he would answer.

"She's coming through here next, and a person would naturally wonder what you think. She a popular writer, you a . . ." Looply smiled, in what may have been a getback for the put-on, smiled just for the fraction of a second before finishing, "A literary one." But the barb had gone home, as though Looply had audibly said what he obviously thought: "And you a writer nobody reads."

Peckham's life hung in the balance, had he but known it. Undreamt by himself, his future was sealed in the single word he was powerless to repress in the flare of rage that, for a fragment of a second, consumed him. Half a lifetime of frustration was discharged in a syllable.

"Trash."

The tape recorder went out with the word locked in its entrails, a javelin in return for a barb, and that barb not even uttered by the javelin's victim, or even by Looply who had, with his tight little grin, merely implied it. Even as Looply went out the door, clutching his machine and the scrap of juicy copy it guaranteed, Peckham realized he had been ungallant with a woman he didn't even know. He wrestled with his conscience the rest of the afternoon, finally phoning the newspaper office with the intention of recanting the judgment, or at least modifying it to something like "She's not my dish of tea." But Looply had already gone for the day, his paltry copy hammered out and probably already in type.

Sleep was a can of maggots. This time Poppy McCloud was trying to get into Manderley, where she knew Peckham was hiding, the iron gate at last giving way as it had to Rebecca-Fontaine. Both women became merged into one pursuing female who cornered him at last, cringing half-soused from wine guzzled in what was famed as the countryside's best cellar—a pun it would take no Dr. Auslese to see through. When he awoke, his mouth felt as if it had been to a party without him, and his eyes looked like dormant bugs. His tongue seemed to weigh as much as the sole of a boot; he was afraid to put it out for fear of being unable to recall it.

But a good breakfast of orange juice, ham and eggs and strong coffee had him feeling a little better, at least with the courage to open the morning paper. He found the interview happily buried near the back, but the word "trash" hit him in the eye like a dart. He read no more than that. He paid his bill, got into his car, and headed rapidly into the west, soon all but healed of his wounds by the gloriously sunlit fertile fields of Iowa, stretching any which way you looked, it seemed, into the open arms of infinity itself. Yet there was always a stain on the horizon. How tangled the skein of human events! And as cause and effect wind their tortuous way, one can but vainly deplore the inequitable distribution of credit and blame, punishment and reward. Life was indeed unfair. The overly Algonquinized Poppy McCloud had got it in the neck because of Dogwinkle's peanut-butter-and-jelly sandwiches and Hostess Twinkies, an upshot for which Peckham could not quite find it in his heart to forgive that scavenging scribbler, Looply.

SIX

Just why the Omaha bookstore next marked for surveillance was called The Evening Breeze was a secret the proprietor would no doubt take to his grave, and soon, too, judging from his appearance. The only thing upright about him at eighty or so was a bristle of white hair like a fright wig, as though he had at some time put his finger in an electric socket with permanent results. As he bustled about the shop his bent figure seemed to topple forward and then catch itself at the last split second, so that he appeared to remain on his feet only by dint of the locomotion itself. Thus he followed the principle of an earth-circling satellite, his forward trajectory being just sufficiently greater than the force of gravity to keep him in orbit. Peckham watched him through the window from the street where, in order to gain access through the door, he had to take his place in a queue of customers lined up for the autographing discovered to be in progress on the day he turned up to check on *Sorry Scheme*.

Break Slowly, Dawn was in any case in plentiful supply, filling one of the store's two large windows, the other of which was hung with a blowup of Poppy McCloud. Curiosity to get a close look at the original outweighed any other emotion Peckham felt at this climax to the progressively swelling crescendo of outrage that was his current life. The authoress (a word like *poetess* that as a feminist sympathizer he normally detested but willingly employed here) sat at a table facing the front of the store, so that he could catch at least intermittent glimpses of her among the sheep shuffling forward for her signature. She wasn't quite as good-looking as her picture (who ever is?) but certainly pretty enough, and not many years older than the twenty-five or so when the picture had been taken. Peckham's outrage having peaked out, as the insipid expression had it, there was no additional degradation in shuffling forward with the sheep lined up outside, moving forward toward the door inch by inch. And he welcomed the chance to talk to a few of this mass-buying breed. He recalled Auden's once remarking how one "somehow never met" any of these apparent millions who read popular authors like Lloyd C. Douglas and the rest. Well, here was a chance to scrape up however fragmentary and ephemeral acquaintance with one or two, to say nothing of an opportunity to brush up on one's rag chewing.

"Have you read that yet?" he asked the elderly woman directly behind him, who was clutching a copy of the book she had come to have signed.

"Oh, yes. I think she's splendid. Have you?"

"Not quite all the way through," he thought it simplest to reply. "What did you think of it?"

"Very absorbing. You're really drawn into the story.

And the characters are so vivid. They stand out so. She knows people."

"I'm told you have to, to get published these days."

"Yes, you do hear of so many books that later became hits, huge successes, that were rejected by publisher after publisher. I read somewhere that *Break Slowly, Dawn* made the rounds for three years before the, let me see, yes, the eleventh publisher accepted it. And then *zzzt*, straight to the top."

"That so. I hadn't known that."

Hmm. Interesting. So ten publishers had shown some editorial acumen before his own had committed the lapse from taste, and the rest history. Add to this the fact that, as one repeatedly heard, many bestsellers were far from read clear through after their follow-the-pack purchase by the owners, and all might not be as dismal as feared. "I got this far through it" and "I've read this much," people were heard to say, measuring off with thumb and forefinger an inch, or even half an inch, of some fat historical romance topping the charts, proving the country wasn't the total cultural desert suggested by their willingness to plunk down $14.95 or $22.50 just to stay in the herd graze.

He began again to take hope. Socked with the realization that an autographing party for the ubiquitous Poppy McCloud was in progress here just when he turned up, Peckham had felt the wind going out of his sails. But now the coincidence braced him as something classically preordained. There was a certain Greek inevitability in their destinies intersecting here in darkest Omaha. A slight rain began to fall, but though it wet his clothes it could not dampen his spirit. He would meet the enemy face to face and with a quickened heart, however outwardly bedraggled. The summer shower let up almost as soon as the woman behind him opened up an umbrella, offering him shelter with her.

"So what you say must have a lot of truth to it," she said.

"What was that?" Peckham asked, having in his musings lost the thread of their conversation.

"That you have to have connections."

"Yes. There's an old Etruscan proverb. It isn't what you know, or even who you know, but what you know about who you know, and even then, what with moral standards ever more relaxed, the scandal threshold becomes increasingly more elevated, so that what once sufficed as influence leverage may not nearly in a time of ethical dilapidation—"

"We can get through the door now."

The orbiting old man's chipper woman assistant was letting the sheep in six or eight at a time, and Peckham was admitted with a cluster of whom the lady behind him was the last. The queue was retidied inside, and now he saw that he was about twentieth or so from the actual table at which Poppy McCloud sat enthroned, smiling as she scribbled away on the flyleaves held open for her, pausing to exchange a few words for as long as any customer wished to protract them. After shifting from one foot to the other for about five minutes, thanks to one man apparently bent on dilating forever his praise of the volume, Peckham suddenly left the line and took up the pursuit for which he had originally come, the quest for *Sorry Scheme*.

Of course he must leave the line, what else? How could he have been so stupefied by developments as to have remained in it as long as he had, as a means of meeting the enemy? He had no book in hand to offer up for signing, and he certainly wasn't going to buy one from the stacks available beside the table. What would he say after poking along to the front? "I'm Earl Peckham, I want to tell you how much I enjoyed plowing through your book"? So he helped himself to a cup of the harmless pink punch available from a bowl in the middle of the shop and, thus armed, began to wander among the shelves and counters looking for himself. At last the old man came toppling forward in his direction.

"Are you looking for anything in particular? Can I help you?"

"I'm Earl Peckham. I was wondering if you had a copy of my novel, *The Sorry Scheme of Things Entire*."

"I . . . think . . . I'm not exactly . . ."

He was flabbergasted to hear Poppy McCloud's own voice ring out from near where they stood. She looked over, smiling brightly. Then she dropped her pen, rose, and walked the few steps over toward them.

"Hey, what a pleasure," she said, extending her hand. "I loved *Sorry Scheme*. Bert Dogwinkle sent it to me, so no royalty in it for you, sorry to say. But if you have a copy in the store," she went on to the proprietor, "I'd like Mr. Peckham to inscribe it to an aunt of mine I want to send it to. She's in the hospital."

The young woman assistant walked briskly to a nearby counter and plucked it out. "We happen to have one copy left."

It looked a little shopworn to Peckham, as though many browsers had handled it without ultimate purchase, but Miss McCloud took it happily and led Peckham, simpering like a schoolboy being awarded a term prize at graduation, to the table for him to autograph. "This is Mr. Earl Peckham," she said to the crowd, "he's written a very good novel which I heartily recommend." She wagged it in midair for all to see before setting it down again, open to the flyleaf. "It's to Melba Wilson," she instructed, "and then anything else you want. Even 'speedy recovery' if you want, because she's in for an operation."

Peckham's own recovery was not so speedy, after scrawling in what he had been told, but as he handed it back to her he did manage to stammer out something reciprocal about having enjoyed *Break Slowly, Dawn.*

"Nonsense. It's not your dish of tea."

"No, I did. It has a very strong plot, and the characters are vividly realized. You know people," he added, figuring he might as well be hanged for an imbecile as well as a liar. Then they stood facing each other in a sort of tremulous mutual embarrassment, grinning somewhat vapidly in each other's face. He found himself piercingly aware of this—relatively—young woman. Slightly under medium height, she had a crop of tight blond curls that resembled a mass of pine shavings, and that one knew sprang back into shape of their own accord the instant she stepped out of a shower, taken in tandem or alone. The same small cherry mouth that denied her beauty guaranteed her prettiness, while suggesting all the snugger envelopment elsewhere, given the erotic legend dear to males that the two orifices are counterparts in size. Such things can vaporize objection.

"Well. I must get back to my . . ."

"Perhaps we can have a drink later."

"Oh, swell. I'd like to talk to you. That would be swell. I'll be here till . . ." She looked to the proprietor and his assistant, who were both standing nearby, agog over this colloquy.

"It's four now," the old man said. "It would be nice if you could stay for the reception till, oh, five, five-thirty. Both of you, of course. You're welcome too, Mr. Packman. The mare the morrier." He was evidently given to Spoonerisms, which is always nice. At eighty, he did not correct himself, having probably not even noticed the merry gaffe.

"No, thank you very much, you're very kind, but I do have an engagement. Suppose I come back around five-thirty."

At the bookstore, Peckham had noticed that throughout her enthronement the short queen had chewed, gnawed, sucked, bitten and what not on the cap of the ballpoint pen with which she did her signing. It had been rarely out from between her teeth except when removed to exchange a few words with a customer. Now in the nearby bar into which they'd slipped for the appointed drink she did the same thing with the swizzle stick from her old-fashioned, removing it only to hold up her end of the conversation.

"I'm trying to quit smoking," she explained. "Grrr." And pretended to claw his shirtfront across the table to illustrate the nervous strain she was under. "I've tried everything, including hypnosis, and a week ago I quit cold turkey. They say the first week is the hardest but I'm afraid it's the first hundred years." She nodded at his virgin Mary. "What's with you and the bloody bores? You an alcoholic? If so I'll trade."

"No, just recovering from a siege of hepatitis. Prohibition is repealed the fifteenth for me. On the wagon nine months to the day. I had a hell of a case of it. We nearly lost me."

"Oh, dear. We did?"

He nodded. He tested her where Mrs. DelBelly had failed. "Nothing like hepatitis to give you a jaundiced view of life."

"Llllove it," she laughed. Couldn't have come through with colors more flying, as Mrs. DelBelly had once remarked in another connection. This was an intelligent young woman, and a merry sprite into the bargain. Under all the surface merriment you knew there was the hot heart. He must navigate very carefully through the shoals of this incipient relationship.

"But I've followed doctor's orders absolutely, much as I've missed those two or three preprandial martinis as you do your cigarettes. He says I can have my first the fifteenth. That's a week from today. Hope we can have it together."

She sucked on the muddler a moment, looking off into

space, before removing it and exhaling a cloud of imaginary smoke. "My husband could work his mouth pretty good too. He once used 'postprandial' in connection with some remarks he had to make at a business banquet, so he had to explain to me what it meant. You're putting me on the same way, aren't you, because I mean nobody could be that, I mean *stuffy*. I learned *postprandial* means after dinner, so *preprandial* means 'before dinner.' "

"I've always wondered. Uh, you say your husband 'could' something or other. Past tense. I hope he's not . . ."

"No, no. I meant my ex-husband. It turned out he swang both ways, but that's another subject. I've had lots of preaching and done a lot of soul-searching as a three-packs-a-dayer, but it's Aunt Melba—the one you autographed the book to?—who brought me up short. A warning. So I guess you know what she's in the hospital for."

"I hope she'll be all right."

"She's a tough cookie, and I do love her. I went to church and prayed for her this morning, and me not even a believer. I mean I'm an atheist with leanings toward agnosticism."

"The big Maybe. I kind of hedge my bets too. Who'm I going to have that big drink with on the fifteenth? Like where will you be?"

"Denver."

"Now there's a coinkidinky. Plan to be there myself then."

He was mad. Stark, staring mad. Did he have this creature in his blood already, that he was prepared to head further west just to see her instead of turning smack around tomorrow as he had planned? He was going round the bend. That it might be fulfilled what was spoken by the prophets, that Peckham should have his marbles examined. But he was on tenterhooks for her response. Why didn't she give it?

Her gaze had been turned momentarily away, as if in some abstraction induced by the subject of her schedule. She jerked her face toward him again. "That would be nice. I'm sorry. I was thinking about something else. I must phone Aunt Melba tonight. Yes, that would be nice. So you're going to Denver, too! I gathered you were on some sort of cross-country gad."

"That's just it, you see. Where the wind listeth."

"You're afraid I'll bite this thing in half." She opened her bag and took out of it a paper napkin in which were wrapped three or four small pepperoni sausages. She began gnawing one as though *it* were the temptation to which she was succumbing. He took one from the extended handful to keep her company. "Don't know whether you've ever been up against a cigarette kicker before, but we smoke anything we can get our hands on. Pencils, pens, sticks of horehound, name it. I even smoke French fries before I eat them. And we eat everything smoked or smokey we can find in the icebox. Smoked salmon, smoked Gouda cheese. Anything that approximates the taste."

A childhood memory that he hadn't recalled for years suddenly sprang into Peckham's mind.

One summer Sunday afternoon, just about this time of year, when he was a boy of ten or eleven, he had stolen up behind his grandfather, the hoo-boying one, as he sat chatting with a crony in the garden. They had been trading amorous recollections, no doubt replete with braggadocio, and the crony was saying, "You want to know what? Get yourself a woman who's trying to quit smoking. The channels the craving will take! You savvy?"

"I savvy."

"I mean she'll smoke anything available. Are you sure your're reading me, Jimbo?"

"Oh, I'm reading you. You don't have to draw me any pictures. The substitute the craving will take. Had the kind of experience you refer to myself once, in spades. Ah hoo boy."

The lad eavesdropping in the summer garden hadn't understood in the least what they were talking about, the lewd old codgers. It took thirty years for the flash of comprehension to strike the grown man sitting in a bar with an all but strange woman who had ignited the spark of memory. The moment must have brought an unconscious smile to Peckham's lips, because Poppy McCloud said, "What? What's so funny?"

"Nothing. Nothing, certainly, about kicking nicotine. I just have this picture of you in one hotel after another phoning room service to send up something smoked. Forgive me. Uh, is Denver your only stop?"

"No, I have three more before that, two of them TV interviews. Oh, and one radio interview."

"They can be murder." Peckham's heart sank at the memory of his own. And it was beating hard when he said, "It would be nice to have that drink with you."

"If you're really going to be in Denver then, swell. Like nothing better."

Hopes that they might become more than drinking companions flared wildly within him.

With her third old-fashioned before her and a fresh muddler in the side of her mouth like a politician's cigar, he was emboldened to ask, as though she had been plying herself with liquor on his behalf, whether they mightn't continue this on into dinner. The Algonquinized, Lutèced and Four-Seasoned commercial star responded with a smiling shrug, hesitated a moment, and said, "Sure. But I should run up to my hotel and shower."

"The same here. Perhaps if we met somewhere at, say, eightish." Christ how he hated that fake-chic little suffix. What was it doing on his lips, even in the cause of airily feigned nonchalance?

"My hotel has a good restaurant. Good room service too. Eight it is then."

Fears that sales of five large printings since publication date, totaling 187,000 copies (exclusive of Book-of-the-Month Club), and five months at the top of the bestseller list would emasculate Peckham proved groundless, while expectations that nicotine craving that keen must find substitute appetitive outlets did not. She seemed to race him in shucking down, flinging garments in every direction. Events moved swiftly to a climax. He drew her to him, crushing her like a pale flower to his breast. His passion seemed to convert itself into a torrent of substandard prose as he mentally articulated what they physically enacted. Their lips met in a kiss. He drank the nectar of her woman's springtime as from a chalice upturned in blissful offer of itself. Then Peckham knew a great peace— or rather, knew that it awaited him in the coming calm of passion spent. A peace already deep within his breast, as it were, kept in promise within his very hammering heart, on deposit for a new tomorrow, one hitherto undreamt. The rustle of their feverishly parted sheets was like a zephyr in the garden of their burgeoning love. Then again it was her breast, no, breasts, now crushed to him, but only till her mouth had drunk its first fill from his, before traveling southward, biting his neck, his shoulders, while her crimson talons drew pink welts along his back, panting as she moved ever downward, downward, until ah hoo boy. The geezers in the garden had been right.

She fell asleep with her tousled head on his own quieted breast, a knee flung across his loins. He dropped off into dreamless slumber himself at last, awakening some time in the middle of the night. She lay away from him now, her back to him, breathing deeply and peacefully. He extricated himself slowly from the bedsheets and walked to the window. It was still dark, but there were vague streaks of light in what was visible, across the rooftops, of the east. Now he murmured something that left him unable to credit the testimony of his ears. He said gently: "Break slowly, dawn."

He lay down again, shaking his head in utter disbelief.

II

SEVEN

It was with a light heart that Peckham stepped along the sunlit street to his Denver rendezvous with Poppy McCloud. His spirits had rarely been higher. Here he was having his long-awaited first drink with an enchantress whose nature and charms he could not possibly have foreseen, his life so far having possessed no precedent, in a city likewise new to him which he found equally exhilarating. She wasn't driving herself, but she had declined his suggestion that they motor out from Omaha together, preferring no distractions while she concluded the strains of this promotion tour—into which her publisher's publicity woman had wedged two additional book-and-author luncheons. This was their first meeting since Omaha. They had kept up by telephone as Peckham rambled about the West on his own, mumbling the vaguest possible information about what he was up to professionally, but agreeing with her that the supplementary botherations of authorship were wearisome indeed. He had talked with her the previous evening from Aspen and made this cocktail date to meet in the bar of her hotel.

He could hardly contain himself when he walked in and found her sitting alone in a booth, smiling across the otherwise empty room. "Yahoo!" he said, or uttered some such ecstatic outcry, twirling his crushproof tweed hat on one finger before pitching it, unsuccessfully, at a rack hook. He hurried over to embrace her before bothering to pick it up. He swung her around in a bear hug, kissing her repeatedly before setting her down on the floor again. Having got his hat on the peg, he slid in across from her. Both her hands in his, he called their order over to the barman, there being no waiter at this off-hour, three o'clock in the afternoon.

"An old-fashioned and a dry gin martini."

"I'm sorry, sir."

"What?"

"I can't serve you." The barman continued what he'd been doing, which was wiping the bar with a damp cloth.

"Why not?"

"You've had enough."

"What the hell are you talking about?"

The bartender swept the cloth across the bar, his eyes lowered.

"You've obviously had more than enough, and we've got to be careful. I mean it behooves us. They're cracking down harder on this thing about keeping a customer to his limit. We're liable, you know, in case of any accident or something befalling. Legally."

"What the hell are you talking about? And what's with all this behooving and befalling? Who do you think you are?"

"I think I'm a man with legal liabilities. There was a suit here only the other week. A tavern served a drunk one too many and is being sued for what happened, which I won't go into the gory details."

"Well, there are going to be some gory details here too, if you pull this thing in reverse and *refuse* to serve somebody who's completely sober. This young woman will testify to that. Aren't I?"

Peckham turned to Poppy for support, but she was holding a hand to her lowered head, shaking with laughter. "I—this man—he's absolutely—" she began, in Peckham's support, but collapsed again in helpless mirth. "Let's go somewhere else."

"No. I mean to make a case of this. If you don't serve me, I'm going straight to the police, have one of those breathalyzer tests, take the results back to you, and make you observe your legal obligation by serving a customer who asks to be served."

Poppy had by now got at least partial control of herself and turned again to the bartender.

"He's right. This man has had hepatitis and hasn't had a drink in—What is it, Earl?"

"Nine months."

"Nine months. That's why he's acting this way. He's so elated by the prospect of his first drink again, by the doctor, you know, allowed by the doctor, that, well, you can honestly say he's intoxicated by the experience itself."

"Look at this hand." Peckham extended one. "Steady as the *Mauretania*."

"Steady as the what?" the barman asked.

121

"Oh, never mind." It had just come to mind as something Noël Coward said at some point in *The Scoundrel*, when emphasizing his stability. "It's a ship. Or was. Let's go somewhere else. To hell with this sobersides."

He rose, plucked his hat off the peg, and led the way outside. Poppy continued laughing from time to time as they made their way down the street to another tavern, where Peckham made a point of composing himself as they walked in. "I like an intellectual who can act like a kid again when it's the right moment," Poppy said, and broke out into a fresh spasm. But presently they were seated together again in a booth, his anger and her hilarity both under control.

When their drinks were delivered, he looked at his a moment as though it were the Holy Grail. "Even normally, there's nothing like that first ice-cold, razor-edge sip of a martini. But *now*. Cheers, my love. And may there be many more together."

"Many more."

His glass being brimful, he raised it very carefully so as not to spill a drop. They sipped together, gazing happily into one another's eyes. Then "Ah!" he whispered, as though giving thanks to the gods.

It was fool's luck that for some reason he had brought the title to his car along, on the chance he might for some reason need it to pick the car up in Cleveland, so there was no trouble selling the Chevy in Denver and flying back with Poppy, who had to get back to her home in Gladwyn, New York, and hadn't the leisure for a cross-country return. Frankly, he needed the money to fatten his thinning wallet, but he didn't tell her that, preferring to let her believe this was all a wild abandon dictated by his need not to leave her side again, which after all had some truth to it. So later that very afternoon he sold the Chevy to a self-declared used-car madman for eighteen hundred dollars cash, to be handed over the following morning the minute the banks opened. Then after another night together in Poppy's hotel room they packed up and flew back to New York—and the light of common day, or as it is sometimes called, the real world.

The plan they more or less agreed on was that they would live together in Gladwyn while keeping his Village apartment as a pied-à-terre, the latter available to both together or for either singly in any arisen need to get away from the other. Simultaneously stimulating and troubling to Peckham was the fact that landing in Gladwyn brought him full circle back near Dappled Shade again. The place was only a few miles away, and who was to say he mightn't run into any of the old bunch. Old bunch! He had left it less than six weeks before but it seemed like years ago, in keeping with the power of sensational occurrences to confer the illusion of time passed. Also, who was to say he mightn't use a session or two to air his dreams with Dr. Hushnecker or Dr. Auslese. For after a period of relatively restful sleep they began to recover something of their former turbulence. For if it wasn't quite yet back to Dappled Shade, it was back to Manderley again.

Instead of the massive furniture around which in times past he'd had to make his way, the great hall now seemed to contain a colossal printing press that spewed out editions by the thousands, under which he was all but buried alive. They were both hardcover and paperback reprints, the latter in quantities naturally proportional to seven-figure advances. He had no more than made his way out of such an avalanche than he was trampled nearly to death by hordes of people trying to buy them, and in one of the more fluid transitions of his dream history a simple revolving drugstore paperback rack became the medieval torture kind on which he was stretched out by masked figures whose particular cruelty was to read aloud to him sales figures other than his own. "A first edition of fifty thousand sold out before publication . . . Two million five hundred copies now in print . . . Half a billion worldwide . . ." The real Manderley consumed by fire in both the book and the movie was reconstructed on the grounds of Dappled Shade, renamed Dappled Sunshine. To gardeners, of course the terms are interchangeable, both meaning the same thing. In fact he remembered one afternoon when he had been trying to learn to chew the rag with Miz DelBelly and Miz Peptide, the former had told them that when the place had been first opened there had been an argument about which to name it, Dappled Shade being agreed on because it was the more common way of putting it. "There was a play called *Dancing in the Checkered Shade* some years ago," he'd told them. "Title is from a line of Milton's, of course, but I can't seem to recall the playwright."

"I'll have my brother-in-law check into it," Mrs. Peptide offered. "He's into the theater."

"That won't be necessary. I just remembered it was John Van Druten."

"We should all be dancing in the checkered shade," Mrs. DelBelly said, drawing a silk handkerchief through her fist and giving it a flutter in the air, to suggest Dionysian abandon.

"Naked as jaybirds."

"Why, Mr. Peckham. I'll tell Dr. Hushnecker on you."

"Praise waits for thee in Zion."

Details of the memory rattled loosely around in Peckham's head, like pellets to be maneuvered into their proper holes in a puzzle box, as he lay trying similarly to reassemble the chimerical particulars of his dream. We are all surrealists at bottom. Well then. He'd had the vivid sensation of being awakened by the printing press roaring on the premises in which he "slept." But as the confusion cleared, like water on the surface of a slime-laden pond momentarily disturbed, he realized it was the sound of Poppy's typewriter going like a submachine gun in her study overhead. She was at work again like the very devil of proliferation. She'd hammered out fifty pages of her new novel in three days. Peckham had in the same period written two sentences, each more exquisite than the other. The specter that had stalked him from the start of this relationship—that this small woman's gargantuan output would castrate him into a writer's block—that very fear itself seemed to be proving self-fulfilling. While Poppy churned the stuff out by the yard, a day's output for Peckham verged on what it might for Flaubert, changing a comma to a semicolon, and reverting to the comma the next. Again dreaming as industriously as some people worked, Peckham slept poorly; sleeping poorly, he needed more rest; so here he was a slugabed at 11:00 A.M. cowering under the thunder overhead. Among the incidental presents he had given Poppy had been something called a Kil-Klatter, a hairy sort of pad like a rectangle made of compacted caterpillars, to set her typewriter on, a product designed to muffle reverberations such as those descending along her metal typewriting stand and thence downward through the original floorboards, but having very little such effect. He must get her a thick shag rug or two to set the stand itself on, that might help. He'd tried to persuade her to get rid of the typewriter stand itself, since its metal construction provided a good deal of the tympani drilling holes in his head, but she had your writer's superstition about parting with something on which she'd turned out her first big hit. It was her lucky piece, bane though it might be to another's existence. But he quite understood the obsession. He still had the paper clip that had accompanied his first check for a short story.

The thunder stopped. There were fainter sounds up there, a rustling, a creaking, then he heard her slowly descending the stairs, and then he sensed her standing in the bedroom doorway, watching him. Not merely, in a fine Faulknerian nuance, looking at him—watching him. The moment was instinct with her vigil. He lay with an arm flung across his eyes, feigning sleep, as she knew very well he was. Was this the moment he had from their very inaugural raptures in Omaha foreseen, and dreaded? When she would come clutching the first new batch of manuscript for him to read? The cloud on the horizon no bigger than a man's hand had scudded inevitably closer, growing as it did. What would he do? Be honest and retain his self-respect, or lie and keep the peace?

The way she cleared her throat told him everything. He let his arm flop away from his brow and muttered something designed to sustain the shabby fiction that he had been asleep, but was now awake.

"Whassamahwa? Timezit?" He raised up on one elbow and blinked hypocritically at the clock, as though he didn't know in advance he would exclaim in surprise at its being eleven o'clock. "Good God."

He hauled his eyes toward the doorway where she still stood, holding a wad of manuscript nearly an inch thick.

"Christ."

"I'll fix us some brunch, good plate of ham and eggs for you, and then you might like to read what I've got so far."

"Oh, swell. Of course it's always a little tricky to show something we've got in the oven. I mean some writers are superstitious about mentioning so much as the title before the thing's complete." He mumbled some names as his feet fished about for his slippers. "Hemingway. Ibsen."

"I'm not Hemingway or Ibsen," she said, and stepping into the room long enough to set the pages on the dresser, she danced away down another flight of stairs to the kitchen to fix the brunch. It had been futile to mention how he hated the word.

He walked naked into the bathroom, muttering a line from Eliot. "I would meet you upon this honestly." From "Gerontion," wasn't it? As he turned on a tap from which to splash his face with cold water he said, "How we pay. And pay. And pay. Verily, thou shalt not go hence till thou hast paid the last farthing." He still worked his mouth pretty good, for all that his tongue still felt mired in Dogwinkle's peanut butter. Why didn't she show the manuscript to *him*? At the Algonquin, over a course of white asparagus. He'd love it, already in spirit banking the do-re-mi.

But of course this was his baby, the dilemma he'd asked for with the first ecstatic clasp in Omaha, and for which he had all along since been steeling himself: lie in your teeth or lose your little paradise. He tried in the few minutes' reprieve left him to get his mind on more pleasant matters. How were things at Dappled Shade? Was Mother Nature still there? Only on days when it wasn't raining cats and dogs were you absolved from the expected compliment, under pain of badmouthing. He had once remarked that the evening was spread out against the sky like a patient etherized upon a table, and she had started a rumor that he'd had an operation and been left permanently unbalanced by the anesthetic. Was the sandwich still stuck in the privet? Or was it a rhododendron? How quickly we forget. Did Mrs. DelBelly marry Dr. Hushnecker and Binnie her Dempster? Was anyone cutting the pages in the beautiful sets of books in the library? It was with that association that a name surfaced for which he had been fishing his brain in vain for months. What writer had answered the question "Who is the greatest French poet?" with the reply, "Victor Hugo, alas"? Of course. André Gide. He had put the query to himself when preparing an anthology. Now at least Peckham had disobsessed himself of *that* one, if there was such a junk word.

His mouth again felt as though it had been to a party without him, returning home around three, maybe three-thirty. His tongue, in the medicine-chest glass, was like a slice of spoiled tongue, and his eyes were tough stains. Love certainly conquered all, and, he reminded himself sternly, you do love this sprite. She is pizzicato on your heartstrings. He shuddered at the cutesy, and went on as best he could.

Drawing on a bathrobe, he stole a glance at the manuscript on the bureau-top to see if it had a title, at the same time trying not to read it if it did. He steeled himself even for that. No title page. Good. The new, and fifth, title for his own work-in-progress, which was progressing like a centipede wearing overshoes, was *Writhing Spaghetti*. That would fix Dogwinkle! He would give him lunch at a Bagel Nosh on that. Yes, it was a rhododendron, he remembered now.

He sat on the edge of their great double bed, at last succumbing to the temptation to fall backward on it. Just for a moment. Climbing into it the first time, he'd remembered Dylan Thomas's rather acerbic comments on the prevalence of the twin bed in contemporary America, as somehow indicative of a lack, or dilapidation, in marriage here. That rolling Dionysian would understandably have disliked the niggardly twin bed. Peckham wondered whether he oughtn't shave before going down. It was somehow disrespectful toward a woman to turn up at breakfast covered with stubble, at least one you weren't married to. And it would give him a few more minutes' reprieve. But as he felt his chin he heard Poppy calling up the stairs, "Ready, baby!" He rose, the bedsprings groaning for him, and descended, knotting the thong of his robe.

She herself was in scarlet espadrilles and the plain blue silk pajamas in which, also by force of superstitious habit, she worked in her attic study, with its steeply pitched ceiling and low windows, an air conditioner practically under the eaves. The pajama coat was open, giving glimpses of her apple-sized, apple-hard breasts as she dished the food up from the stove to the table. It was a country-style kitchen, with high, deep-silled windows brightened with flowered chintz curtains. Coming down, Peckham had bumped his head on one of the original beams installed by the previous owner, and he was grateful for the contusion of his brow which he was free to feel as a distraction from the general air of nervousness prevailing.

"A goose egg from an original beam always has more tone," he said, and she laughed with a nervous excess, indicating both the writer's anxiety over a new work being given its first tryout with a human response, and a wish to butter up the reader as an aid to acquiring his good opinion. They both knew the joke lay in the beam's false pretenses: it was about as "original" as the new flashing put around the chimney a few years before. "Those floorboards in your study creak all right, though, when you walk around on them."

"They're the McCoy," she said, shoveling some ham and eggs onto his plate. "And oak." She darted about like a dragonfly, pouring orange juice and coffee, fetching popped toast, jam, salt and pepper, and pausing now and then to "smoke" one of the pork sausages she had with her own eggs, before eating it. Sometimes it would hang out of the side of her mouth like an actual gasper as she affected a deep drag on it, even going through the motions of inhaling as a preface to actual consumption. She polished off six or eight in this way. The dangling mock cigarette, together with her half-nakedness, gave her a dissolute air that was also touching, as though she were a girl playacting at being a wanton in a game of grown-up. He sensed her trying to study his face for signs that he had read at least a few pages and some hint of what impression they might have made. To put her mind at rest he said, "I'm dying to get to it. As soon as I take the car down for the oil-and-lube job. It needs it. Those Mercedes have to be babied, you know. I mean it's your car. I can easily walk back."

"Oh, I'll do that. I need the walk more than you do. Besides, I have some shopping to do, and he should have it ready by the time that's finished. Aren't you impressed that I wrote over twenty thousand words without falling off the wagon? A day at the typewriter usually meant a pack. That was when I needed it most. I seem not so theatening to climb the walls now. No, you stay home and curl up."

That was hardly his first priority once she was out of the driveway. Having from the window watched her wind away in the yellow convertible, he ran like hell up the two flights of stairs to her study, where he began rummaging frantically through her mail in search of the latest batch of stuff he knew she'd got from her clipping bureau. Writers who said they never read reviews were generally liars—he was one himself—but Poppy was true to her word, at least had been after the first few, which had been unfavorable. All of which put her commercial triumph in the crying-all-the-way-to-the-bank category. Peckham wasn't interested in the new notices. He wanted to see whether the fresh sheaf of cuttings contained the newspaper report of the interview in which he'd called her stuff trash—for the clipping bureau in question was nothing if not thorough, sending on not merely notices but any scrap of newspaper or magazine print making any mention whatever of the client in question. He found the large manila envelope from the Quincy Publicity Bureau all right, and, true to her claim, she hadn't opened it. His heart sank when he saw that they had not only sealed it with the gummed flap—that he could have steamed open and pasted down again—but had reinforced it with several lengths of crisscrossed Scotch tape. These he could never tear off without leaving the back in tatters. She would have known he'd tampered with it. Damn! So he had to leave the packet where it was, with no certainty that it didn't contain the bombshell whose existence had haunted him from the first of their relationship. When would it detonate? Why did she subscribe to a clipping service if she never read the reviews? "I'll read them later, when it no longer matters," she said.

He crept downstairs like a criminal to his own first-floor study, picking up the manuscript on the way. He threw himself into his armchair and began to read. It began auspiciously—or ominously, if you're a mate in dire dread of being outshone by the little woman.

" 'What a waste of electricity,' Granny said as the lightning flashed about the house. It was the worst summer storm of that year, and soon cut off our own. The last thing we clearly saw before being plunged in darkness was Granny removing her spectacles and setting them on the table beside her knitting so as not to tempt fate by attracting current to their wire frames . . ."

My God, was she going to be good? A tremor of apprehension not unlike Granny's own went through him as he read on, writhing like spaghetti. That opening paragraph he'd have been proud to own himself. It had precision, economy and, yes, wit. Had she been rereading *Sorry Scheme?* Intently? So that he was becoming a major influence on her?

But what started off so well soon gave promise of being another three-generation family saga, lumbering along at the same heavy pace, marred by the same pedestrian laying on of detail as was its five-pound predecessor. It would be another "good read" for summer purchasers to bury themselves in for a season. The resulting verbal obesity, as he had never ceased to call this word plethora to his classes, made for what an editor had called, in a flattering rejection Peckham himself had once got from *The New Yorker*, "a lack of connotative complexity." In other words there was no more than what lay on the printed page, to reverse Willa Cather's definition of a *good* writer—namely someone who gave you more than what was on the page. There was nothing between the lines here, the reader's own imagination was never enlisted—and it would sell another hundred thousand copies.

Poppy didn't return with the car until nearly four o'clock, deliberately leaving him no excuse not to have finished it. He was waiting for her in the garage doorway, grinning broadly in his bathrobe.

"It's great."

"You don't like it."

She walked so fast toward the house that she seemed to be racing him to the kitchen door. Peckham had often found his long legs outstripped by short girls. Possibly taking twice as many steps gave them the advantage. Or maybe they were overcompensating, another word he was fed to the follicles with. In any case, the screen door had closed behind her by the time he had sprung up the porch steps, so that he had to open it again.

"Such richness of detail," he went on, pattering in her wake. "I mean the sheer physical opulence, the broad canvas," he babbled hypocritically on. Anything to keep peace. Some marriages founder on deception, others are founded on it, he thought. Not bad, he must remember to put that down. He felt guiltily for the pad and pencil he always kept in his robe. They had reached the living room and she was pouring herself her usual bourbon and bitters on the rocks. He fixed himself a martini the same way. After a hefty slug, her manner softened a little, as did his heart toward her. Oh, he quite understood the tensions of writers! Writing a book was like a long bout of illness even when somebody *else* was doing it.

Standing in the middle of the floor with her coat open and the drink rattling in her hand, she said, "But with that sacred principle of yours, that less is more, more has to be less. That's what it would amount to if you turned it around."

"No, no, not necessarily—to the new book—not necessarily. There are different kinds of writers. You remember the famous argument between Fitzgerald and Wolfe, about the leavers-out and the putters-in. Scott raised hell with Tom for laying it on with a trowel, and Tom cited Cervantes and Shakespeare as a few who did the same thing."

"But when you told me that story you were on Fitzgerald's side. Then when I put in a word for Wolfe you said, 'Not while I'm eating.'"

"I did?"

"You certainly did. You were sitting right there." She pointed through the open doorway to the dining room table. "So it's a little disingenuous of you to praise in my work what you deplore for your own case."

He shrugged and smiled rather sheepishly. He walked around a long refectory table and dropped into a chair behind it. She took off her coat, dropped it on a sofa, and settled herself in a chair she had to swing around to face him, a leg slung over its arm. They were an almost grotesque recapitulation of his last creative writing class, when the elective seminar had dwindled to one pupil and the university had fired him. That student had also been a young woman likewise given to slouching nonchalantly in her seat—and to the overwriting which Peckham had similarly felt it his obligation to chastise. Poppy seemed in a devilish way to be reading his mind, perched there in a shocking-pink jumpsuit and blue sash. She took another swig of her drink and said:

"Go ahead, make with the oxymoronic. Be cruel in order to be kind."

Peckham had got so that he could lecture without his notes, so deeply had they been burned into his mind over the years. Half a lifetime of teaching rained on Poppy McCloud, his last and reluctant but utterly absorbent class of one. Fiction was the art of stretching truth as far as it would go, but the elasticity consisted of a vibrancy born of concision. "In composing, as a general rule, run your pen through every other word you have written; you have no idea what vigor it will give your style. Sydney Smith. Tell the reader only what he has to know, and let him imagine the rest. Shaw. Make the reader a collaborator in the creative process by——"

The pupil's hand was up.

"Yes?"

"But Shaw himself went on forever."

"We're not Shaw. It depends on who's on the phone. You can be elliptical for half a million words and verbose in a hundred. I was going to——"

"And Eugene O'Neill had this principle. Tell them what you're going to say, tell them you're saying it, and tell them you've said it."

"No friend to the art of omission he!" Peckham answered with a laugh, as though quite sharing with her a facetious recollection of the playwright's own unconscious self-condemnation. "And look where he is today—quite outstripped by Tennessee Williams." Peckham felt the need to pace, always keeping the stout table between them. "I was going to cite Joyce Cary's point, I think it was, if memory serves, about making the reader a partner in the creative process by enlisting his imagination. There's a passage in the very beginning of your book that perfectly illustrates what I'm— Let me just fetch it." That was done in the ten seconds it took to dart into an adjoining alcove serving as his study and snatch the manuscript from the desk where it lay. "I can't tell you how excited I was by the opening, the feeling how good it was," he said, readily alchemizing the fear that it was. "But then there's almost a page about the storm stopping when all you really need to indicate it is this one fine sentence. Here it is. 'Now and then a leaf twitched as a lingering raindrop fell not from the sky but merely from a bough overhead.' That's all we need to know to realize that Granny looking out with her dim eyesight thinks it's still raining when it's just drops falling from the wet trees. The rest is—suet! Cut, cut, cut. I love Granny. Oh, and Uncle Dump. You must do more with Uncle Dump. Wanting to move to the suburbs because he hears about the wife-swapping there and hopes to trade his own in for a fresh bundle of complaints. Heh heh," Peckham went on, himself hoping to recover the evening's threatened peace with some diplomatically extruded laughter. Then his face sobered. "But we seem to have an anachronism here. There was no wife-swapping at the turn of the century when we meet the first of these three family generations. Hmm." He stroked his chin.

"Four. No, that's a flashforward. You know—the opposite of a flashback. It's big these days. Didn't you get that, that it's a flashforward?"

"I guess I missed something . . . Ah, yes, I see." He shuffled through some pages. "Of course. You're anticipating Uncle Dump as the future, and naturally still un-born, grandson of this Cousin Dumphrey. Well, he'll be a scream when he comes along, never you fear. You're certainly painting a broad canvas here, ducks. All the more reason to be as elliptical as possible *in the writing*, don't you see. Less is more, and enough is too much, as the fella said, and so forth and so on. I think you get my point, at least as it expresses *my* opinion about what *I* think is good writing, and which I strive for myself." He shuffled through some more pages. "There are the usual minor things. Mistakes we all make. A spider isn't an insect. It has eight legs, whereas an insect has only six. And it isn't kilts. It's *a* kilt."

"This is a different kind of spider. A period-piece cast-iron frying pan with a long handle and short legs. My grandmother still had one then. It has nothing to do with the insects the family's talking about in that scene. You probably didn't read word for word."

"I was so engrossed in the story qua story. Which rolls on with your usual—solidity. And *enervate* means 'to weaken,' not 'invigorate.' But then lots of people make that mistake. But the main thing is, boil it down." Peckham himself could not have said to what extent rivalry, sexual tension, envy, frustration and plain fear played a part in what he did next, as against the plain moral ob-ligation to tell a loved person the truth. There was also the obligation to himself to summarize what he had been saying as a teacher who had served on the barricades with countless young aspirants for whom it had likewise been his duty to balance consideration with honesty. "The point as I see it is cut, cut, cut," he repeated, hefting the manuscript as though to emphasize its overweight. "Take this out and run the lawn mower over it."

She rose quietly, walked back to the liquor cabinet, poured herself another bourbon over rocks taken with the same deliberation from the ice bucket, and went out of the room. He watched her, still from behind the refectory table that had physically converted this into a classroom. In the doorway to the rear of the house she turned around and came back. She had forgotten something. The manuscript. She picked it up and this time completed her exit.

"Remember, I'd have said the same thing to Wolfe," he called. "And Cervantes and maybe Dickens." He raised his voice. "I mean whoever these days produces or is expected to sit through an uncut *Hamlet* or *Tristan*? Everybody can be cut, so there's no need to feel . . ."

He freshened his own martini to the sound of the kitchen door slammed, followed by footsteps down the back porch stairs. He took his drink into his study, as though it were a ceremonial libation accessory to an observance of the separateness of the parties to any union such as this, sitting down in his leather club chair there with a grave deliberation also part of the rite. From the direction of the garage, through one of the thick walls of this old whitewashed stone house, came sounds that eluded interpretation, except that they had a rapidity and crispness that made him think of the word *huff*. Metallic scraping, some sort of clanking. Then there was the roar of a gasoline motor starting up, followed by the unmistakable rattle of the power cutter. He ran to the kitchen window, half-crazed with the expectation of finding her shredding twenty thousand words of manuscript under the blades of the sit-down mower as his punishment. She was aboard the mower all right, tearing in a rage across the yard, at least to the extent to which that can be done at a speed of three miles an hour. There were no fragments of paper among the neglected late-September grass, but when she made a turn at the far border of the property he could see that her nostrils were snorting smoke from a cigarette hanging from the corner of her mouth. Good God, he had in one moment made her destroy a book and driven her back to nicotine. But with a burst of relief he saw the manuscript lying safely on the kitchen table. That left half of his offense—certainly burden enough. He started to open the door and gesticulate for her attention but thought better of it. Let her work off her steam. There was nearly an acre of unkempt lawn in which to do it. He turned back and finished his martini, listening to the retributive racket of their—or rather her—five-horsepower Jacobsen as it came and went about the yard. But the cigarette made him sick. Three months of self-discipline shot to hell in one second of artistic temperament, a term that gave him a headache. There had been a long drought, and he imagined her shooting her lighted butt into the dry brush at the height of her pique, starting a fire that would consume them as it had Manderley. To distract himself till the terrible confrontation that awaited them, he tried to remember all the other novels he could that had houses burn down in them. *Jane Eyre* of course, *The Spoils of Poynton*, *The Wap-*

shot Chronicle— The phone rang, which he took from an extension installed in his study, presumably to facilitate telling callers that he must not be disturbed.

"Is Poppy there?"

"She's busy now. May I take a message?"

"I don't want to disturb her," said the woman's voice. Peckham wondered whether it was possible to disturb anyone in volcanic eruption and just how you would go about it. "Nothing important. I'll try again later, thanks. You might tell her Juniper Schwartz called."

He returned to his rather frenetic brooding, against that awful *put-putting* background. The grounds urgently needed barbering; the cliché "judicious cutting" which editors used for prolix manuscripts floated to mind. Praise God this one was not in the danger he had at first wildly supposed. But what plea could he cop for the smoking? It looked as though he was going to have to violate his own drinking quota this day, possibly even get a little drunk to get through the awaiting ordeal. On his way for another refill he veered into the kitchen and plucked the manuscript off the table, like someone saving a cub from an animal that destroyed its young.

The racket outside stopped. The screen door creaked open. What were those lines from Emily Dickinson again?

> *What fortitude the soul contains,*
> *That it can so endure*
> *The accent of a coming foot—*
> *The opening of a Door—*

"Where's my manuscript?"

"In a safe place. Or till I can get it Xeroxed and neither of us will have any regrets."

"Christ."

"The mot juste."

He realized that in not instantly apologizing for having made her tear open the pack of cigarettes (kept around like the alcoholic's cautionary bottle of bourbon) and light up, in making no immediate mention of it, he was leaving up to her the decision whether to do so or not. Of course it might prove a one-time thing, but he doubted it. That she had fallen off the tobacco wagon and was due for a smoking binge would more probably prove the case. A sinner's backslide to two or three packs a day, until the next penitent's vow. Then she would again, as she herself put it, "spend every day not smoking."

They had their cocktail hour together, separated only by the wall that divided the alcove-cum-study from the living room, where she herself sat. He eked out what he could of his martini, and more, sucking back drop after drop of the melting cubes in his reluctance to face her by making the trip required for a refill. In turn he could hear the ice clinking in her own glass—she had the advantage of replenishment readily at hand. Then his ear caught quite another sound. The click of a lighter? Yes. Then faintly, but distinctly, the pop of her lips as she characteristically sucked back a mouthful of smoke. There was no end to his perfidy. Each snick of her finger as she flicked ashes into an ashtray was like a nail driven into his guilt. At last the faintest but most easily recognizable noise of all, the butt twisted and crushed out, like his soul. He could stand it no longer. He would gird up his loins, go and beg her forgiveness.

He was heaving his hundred tons of leaden remorse out of the chair when she materialized in the doorway.

"I'm sorry," she said.

He would never understand women. What distressed him was not so much the acknowledged fact but the dismal level of platitude down to which it dragged him—that of the ten million corny hubbies who said, "Can't live with 'em, can't live without 'em." He had a horror of bromide, understandable in one who spent his professional life in a corner, spinning silken subtleties. Yet some of the best writers he "taught" had told us life came down in the end to a handful of clichés. Faulkner in *Intruder in the Dust*, Huxley in what was it again? *Antic Hay, Crome Yellow*? Possibly *Point Counter Point*. He was getting a bit rusty on Huxley, but the line went something like "We come back to truism in the end." Well, here was Earl Peckham chiming in with the ten million corny hubbies, "Can't live with 'em, can't live without 'em." He frequently assigned his creative writing students a short story of Katherine Anne Porter's called "Rope," in which the unpredictability of women was graphically delineated. Not so much for the content as for the economy of space in which it was done—a mere few thousand words. He must have Poppy read it.

"I overreacted."

"It was I who was impolitic."

"Im—what?"

"My choice of words wasn't perhaps the best. I did give you credit for expecting an honest reaction and a straight answer. I always told my students, if I come down hard on something it's because I feel there's something worth coming down hard on."

"Love all those 'hard ons,' " she said, putting her head to his breast, and the way she ran the back of her hand against her cheek told him there were tears in her eyes, even as she laughed. Astonishingly, there was going to be an amorous outcome to all this. He would never understand *people*. Can't live with 'em, can't live without 'em. "It was unfair of me to ask your opinion and then bridle at it."

"No, I could have made my points with more consideration for an author's feelings, being one myself." His horror of banality did not prevent his adding, "It's important to put ourselves in the other fellow's shoes." Wincing, he quickly upgraded his metaphor, if only a little. "To try to get inside someone else's skin."

They embraced, carefully, so as not to dribble on one another from their tintinnabulating glasses.

"There's an old Arabian proverb."

"Not now."

"Darling."

They were silly like that for a bit, warming to a crescendo concluded right smack-dab there on the living room floor, as Uncle Dump would say, a kind of extemporaneity Poppy liked as proof that they were not finding each other an old story but remained mad, mad, do you hear, too animal-urgent to bother waiting to get to bed. Indeed, in the bedroom itself she sometimes preferred the floor for their more quadruped bouts. But as quickly as ignited, they were spent, and sat naked with fresh drinks amid their strewn clothing. Yet this was not to be one of the times when they got stewed, just lounged about with a pleasant buzz on, the critical business of the day far from over, merely winding down to a resolution saner than a short time ago either would have dared hope. She looked seriously across the room at him from her chair.

"Teach me to write."

"Now you're like Hemingway, after all."

"What do you mean?"

"It's what he said to Gertrude Stein when he first presented himself on her doorstep on Rue whatever-it-was."

His stroll about the room brought them back to a classroom juxtaposition, but this time of the more relaxed kind, when Peckham would come from behind his desk as the session thawed down and he would face his students neither quite sitting on it nor leaning against it, but a combination of both. It would not stand between them but would simply be a piece of furniture momentarily supporting him as their chairs did them. They did not the less expect a lecture resumed, nor did Poppy now. And, of course, they were both naked, always a great aid to informality. But squatting tailorwise—or perhaps in some approximation of the lotus position for which she had also in the end lacked the discipline—she was all aglow with attention. The blond thatch just visible past her parted knees was not now too much of a distraction, nor were the sweet little breasts.

" 'Style is a very simple matter,' Virginia Woolf once wrote to Vita Sackville-West, 'it is all rhythm. Once you get that you can't use the wrong words. This is very profound, what rhythm is, and goes far deeper than words. A sight, an emotion, creates this wave in the mind, long before it makes words to fit it,' she goes on to say, and then, let me see if I recall it all, by God, I think I can, practically verbatim. 'In writing one has to recapture this, and set it working, and then, as it breaks and tumbles in the mind, it makes words to fit in.' " He finished it more with the excitement of a pupil who has successfully given a recitation than as a teacher who has remembered a quotation without recourse to notes.

"Aha. Rhythm. I can see that. A sentence should dance, if at all possible. I know I get that sense when I read a good one, or one that satisfies me for some reason. As many do in *Sorry Scheme.*"

"Thank you. You can even call the subject and predicate partners in the measure they tread."

"The qualifying clauses steps!"

"Precisely!" Peckham said, though he felt they were running this thing into the ground. "It may seem that we've now opened an entirely different can of peas from that of the concision we were discussing before. But actually we haven't. Because we know that in a dance there must be no wasted motion. In any case there are two major elements in a work of fiction, especially a novel. Structure and texture. You're all structure. I'm all texture. I know that, I admit it. Yet in a larger sense," he went on, realizing he was beginning to sound like Abraham Lincoln, "in a

146

larger sense form and content are inseparable." From force of habit he held a forefinger oratorically aloft. "*Totally so in poetry, less so in narrative*, but inseparable nonetheless. The grain is the wood, the wood is the grain. Yes?" For she had raised her hand.

"If each of us has something the other lacks, and I admit you knocked my socks off with *that* epiphany, then an amalgamation of the two of us would be something on wheels, right?"

"Right."

She rose, as though she'd heard enough, but in a wholly favorable sense. Her mind was made up. The lesson had been taken to heart.

"My course is clear," she said, sounding a little statesmanlike herself for someone tootling around in the altogether. "I must be more like you. I must fall completely under your sway. I must saturate myself with you, take you in with my pores, fall completely under your sway."

"My dear—"

She ignored him, continuing her march around the room.

"I see now absolutely what you mean. Boil the stuff down, shoot for texture. The 'sedulous ape' theory, wasn't that Stevenson's expression? There's nothing wrong with having influences, every writer does when he first starts out. You must be my influence."

"But there are other masters," he persisted, falling into stride beside her, or at least behind her, as she continued on into the kitchen. It was only to get some snacks, so that it was to the cunning derrière alone visible past the open refrigerator door that he addressed his enumerations. "Flaubert, Waugh, Beerbohm, perhaps Barbey d'Aurevilly—"

"*Who?*" This through a flap of ham hanging from her mouth. "Who he?"

"Never mind. Just somebody I found a turn-on when I was your age."

"I've naturally read some of them, but you're to be my model for the nonce, or time being." She laughingly stuffed a slice of ham between his own teeth. It was a hobby of hers, facetiously poking tidbits into him, sometimes across restaurant tables. "Besides that I'll pick your brains plenty, mister. Oh, you'll pay for my physical favors. This body. It's not voluptuous, I know, but it's got a motor in it." She shoved a few olives into his face and led the way back to the living room, carrying a plate of cold cuts and cheddar cubes prestidigitated from God knows where. There she became serious. Setting the plate on an end table, she held up the ashtray with the telltale twisted stub in it.

"I'm an ex–former cigarette smoker."

"I noticed."

"The hypnosis didn't work. I thought it would."

"Today's little drama blew it. I'm sorry. I was sure you'd kicked it. Do you want to try the hypnosis again? I know it's worked for some people."

"No. Where's my pack of Endits? Maybe I'll try them again. They taste so horrible they *should* make you quit."

"Let me hypnotize you. I've had zum zuccess in zis area."

"O.K., doctor." And she stretched out on the couch, folding her arms on her breast in an attitude of utterly submissive composure.

On a nearby table lay a wristwatch of his with a flexible metal band, plucked off and flung down in his haste to disrobe for their lovemaking. It twinkled brightly as he swung it before her eyes, from a chair drawn up beside the couch.

"Now take a deep breath, close your eyes, restfully, dreamily, that's right, easy, relax completely, give yourself absolutely to sleep. The kind that knits up the raveled sleeve of care. Knits up, knits up, knits up," he repeated with a lulling monotony. And though it had begun as horseplay, he saw to his amazement that she was going under. He set the wristwatch aside on a table and touched her on the shoulder, shaking her gently. But there was no doubt. She was dead to the world.

He rose and paced the floor briefly in a mixture of uncertainty and excitement, fear and the most astonishing sense of challenge. Why not? What could he—they— lose? The feat of mesmerism lay wholly within the patient's willingness, after all, not the physician's powers of domination, though that was not to be ruled out entirely, given the former. Even domination of a—dare he say it of himself?—Svengalian order. Now would be the moment seriously to test an intimation hitherto given only half-humorous consideration. The poor damsel did desperately want to kick cigarettes, especially since her Aunt Melba's pulmonary troubles seemed to have taken a turn for the worse. No, they couldn't lose anything. And who knew what might be gained. If only another few months' reprieve, it would be worth it.

"When I clap my hands three times, you will wake up. But until then you will do exactly as I say. You will decide

149

for yourself that tobacco is as loathsome as it tastes and, more important, tastes as loathsome as in fact it is. Here." He shook one of the truly hideous Endits from the pack she kept in a drawer of the table, lit it with her lighter, and took a drag to get it going well. It certainly lived up to the manufacturer's claim that it should drive any addict to abstention, at least so it seemed to Peckham. When it was burning steadily, he slipped it between her lips and said, "Now take a puff." He lifted her head with his free hand so she might more easily comply. "There. Now inhale . . . deeply, deeply." She coughed and spluttered smoke in a heavy cloud. "There, you see? That's how cigarettes taste, and you will carry the memory of it into your waking life—forever." He had no idea what the regular hypnotists' routines might be like, but this looked hopeful from the faces she made. His own technique, improvised by having the appearance of validity, would be now to transfer the experience of revulsion to a real cigarette, so after punching out the Endit in an ashtray he lighted one of her regulars, also fortunately handy. He repeated the operation, this time saying, "You see how terrible this is?" and trying with his voice and manner both to instill the power of suggestion. "You see? One of your regular so-called low-tar brand, but isn't it as disgusting?" He was rewarded with a grimace as bad as the first, and the smoke was again emitted in a coughing splutter. Things were going well. But he refrained from putting an end to the session quite yet. While he had her under his spell, why not try to extend its fruits to the sphere of her life about which she had just revealed herself to be equally concerned—the professional? She did want to improve and refine her writing, do something more than turn out bestseller potboilers. Why not therefore take this golden opportunity to inculcate her more deeply with the truths he had been trying to emphasize in conscious life. Those values, absorbed profoundly into the unconscious, would be like unto the yeast that leaveneth the whole loaf. He went really to work as Svengali.

As he did so, he found it eerily interesting that the du Maurier who wrote *Rebecca* was a granddaughter of the man who wrote *Trilby*, he, Peckham, being under the curse of the former novel and the spell of the second. But it was only a fleeting thought crossing his mind as he proceeded to the task of seizing an opportunity at once exhilarating and awesome. He would make it a point of honor not to be as sinister with his little Trilby as that shaggily bohemian forerunner had been with his, and certainly he must purge from his mind the memory of Barrymore standing at the window and with his ghastly colorless eyes exerting his powers clear across the rooftops of Paris to the budding singer whose own gifts he would bring to full fruition. And one more thing. There would be no occasion for him to say, as Barrymore had with that forlorn self-disgust as he held in his arms a Trilby hypnotized into amorous response, "My manufactured love." He already had the voluntary affection of his own! Of course in either case the clay was in need of molding, and mold what was entrusted to his tutelage he would strive to do to the best of his own lights. Of course there was the dangerous thrill of playing God.

"When you awaken, after I clap my hands three times, you will have a passion for excellence. You will seek it according to the examples we have agreed on as most conducive to that refinement of substance of which you know your work to be in dire need, and in keeping with counsels of mine which you know you have already voluntarily sought. Pick my brains, then; they are yours for the plucking, like fruit whose any sustenance you are heartily welcome to. But do as I say. Don't listen to people like Dogwinkle, to say nothing of his even more mercenary partner, Dearie, and that scavenging ten-percenter, our mutual agent, Toedink. All they'll want is another commercial blockbuster. They don't know from literary quality. They don't really care. They only keep people like me on to sweeten their lists and to keep them from utter venality. The potential is there," he went on, inadvertently lapsing into still another cliché he found abysmally threadbare, "but it must be developed with a singleness of purpose equal to, but at the same time diametrically opposed to, the mere profit motive of men who are not publishers at all, but only merchants. They manufacture things called books; that exhausts their interests. If my demands seem selfish, they are anything but. For I now freely suspend my own endeavors for the best cultivation of yours. But you must give this in return, must make this vow. To take my advice in your new work in progress, make any corrections and, most especially, cuts I suggest. The purification of your talent must be our first and last consideration. Our joint mission begins as of this moment. When you awaken you will be—*the best Poppy McCloud you can!* Now you may wake up."

She slept on. Not even shaking her by the shoulders did any good. She even developed a light snore, as though the slumber she had slipped into had been a natural progression from the profoundest boredom. She reminded Peckham of the last pupil in his final seminar, a girl roughly the same size and coloring, who had dozed off in the middle of some comments on Henry James's prefaces to his novels. True, she had been on a heavy toot the night before, but even then it had been more than a trifle disconcerting. There might have been a little humorous self-disparagement in the situation, not too dissimilar to Svengali's, as enacted by Barrymore in the sardonic remark about his manufactured love. Peckham might regard himself as having manufactured some tedium for somebody. But when, after shaking Poppy even more briskly, she still showed no sign of coming to, his annoyance turned to apprehension, and that swiftly to panic. He had heard stories about hypnotists' occasional difficulties in bringing subjects to, which might be all the graver for amateurs playing God. He had a terrified vision of Poppy sleeping forever, like a princess in a fairy tale. Crazily, he even bent to kiss her, like the prince appointed to rouse her from what might otherwise have been eternal oblivion. Zilch.

He must seek help. Professional help. Where? Dr. Hushnecker, galling as such an appeal might be. He found the Dappled Shade number in the book and hurriedly dialed it. Dr. Hushnecker was in conference just then. Was this urgent? Desperately. Dr. Hushnecker would be free within the half hour, maybe sooner. Would the caller leave a message and number? No, the caller would be right over, and would buttonhole the doctor personally so as to take no chance on his leaving without being contacted.

Peckham dressed in a rush and, covering Poppy with

an afghan fortunately nearby, tore down the road in the car. The radio had been on when last used, and he let it run now. Some rock group was playing a current hit. Something picked up live from a concert. They were going full blast when Peckham veered up the driveway at Dappled Shade. The song ended with a roar of applause, that segued into a rhythmic clapping, evidently an audience demand for an encore. He parked as near to the main building as he could and dashed up the well-remembered flight of five stairs to the office. He was hurrying down the corridor to Hushnecker's office when he stopped cold, thought, turned around, and galloped back to the car. It was the rhythmic applause that had popped the clue to the surface from his own possibly subconscious mind. Of course. He had forgotten to clap three times, the order given in advance for waking up.

He tried to keep from speeding as he returned. If something happened to him, under whose dominion the princess slept on, she might never awaken. He left the car in the driveway, tore up the stairs and back into the living room. He clapped three times.

"All right," he said breathlessly, "you will now wake up as directed."

She opened her eyes, yawned, and sat up. He sank gratefully to his knees beside the couch and took her hand in both his. Having calmed himself, he told her as systematically as he could what had happened—not that it was strictly necessary if posthypnotic suggestion was all it was cracked up to be. They had a supper improvised from an icebox fortunately loaded with leftovers, and retired early.

The day ended as it had begun, with Peckham's arm flung across his brow, only this time with no fraudulence. He felt as though he had spent the intervening hours being pulled backward through a knothole and wound up with all his molecules violently rearranged. He was grateful to have memory jog him back to some sense of ordinary routine just before he dropped off. He shook her gently by the shoulder.

"Oh, by the way, a Juniper Schwartz telephoned."

"Hm?"

"Juniper Schwartz."

As if from the borderland of her own well-earned rest she mumbled in response: "That's my hypnotist."

EIGHT

"So I'm being Eliza Doolittle to your Henry Higgins."

Peckham kept his little secret with an easygoing smile of acquiescence. It would be best not to reveal that the parallel was rather otherwise than the Pygmalion one she had in mind, however fully she understood that it was hypnosis to which she was responding, and for matters pertaining to more than cigarettes—which she had successfully resisted for more than a month now, a month in which she was going like a house afire at her typewriter, likewise on lines laid down by her gently relentless mentor. Possibly the adventure on which they were now irreversibly embarked was a kind of amalgam of the two literary themes. In no case must it be borne in on her that she was playing Trilby to his Svengali.

He had spotted a subplot in the new book that he thought might be extracted and made into a successful short story. About a husband who is infuriated by money his wife has spent modernizing the kitchen into the old-fashioned farm-type affair then coming into chic vogue, divorces her, and then marries the "idiot woman" who

157

has designed and talked her into the restoration, a modish sort who, after all, he feels is more up his alley. "It's juicy with ironies," Peckham said. "But play it low, cool. Subtle suggestion wins the day, points tangentially made, not obvious explicitness, remember? Try it on *The New Yorker*. They might just go for it. Keep it oblique, not head-on. And don't lay it on with a trowel, your besetting sin," he went on, rather repetitiously for one plugging concision, what? Ho, he knew that. Paradoxically, he had to preach nonpreachment, and the fact was a nettle to his spirit. To have to lay minimalism on with a trowel. But she kept it oblique, with some blue-penciling from him, he liked the postsurgical result, they shot it off to *The New Yorker* and awaited response from the mountaintop.

It was precisely during this aching vigil that his own mail took a vivid turn.

Word of Binnie Aspenwall blew unexpectedly into his life, piquing as much curiosity as it satisfied about what had become of that volatile niece of Mrs. DelBelly's (about whom he wondered in equal measure). Came a letter addressed care of his publisher and forwarded from there, indicating that she had no idea of his own current whereabouts. "Ms. Aspenwall" was typewritten over the return address on the envelope, that of a New York magazine called *Whirligig,* and the contents of the letter left no clue as to whether she had married that Dempster . . . what was his name? Dempster Hyster. Or whether as his wife she might now be living smack around the corner somewhere in these semibosky suburbs.

"Dear Earl," the letter ran, "surprised to hear from me?

Me too. But I've just become poetry editor of *Whirligig*, a new monthly devoted exclusively to entertainment of a high order we hope we hope we hope. I remember from our dear conversations how addicted you are to poetry, and naturally wonder whether perchance you don't also *write* the stuff. Anything in the kettle, or even the trunk? The lighter the better for us. More, well, verse, than poetry. Love to hear from you. Love, Binnie."

It revived the ambivalent, half-exasperated passion he'd felt for Binnie from the first of their acquaintance. On a more practical level, it reminded Peckham of the one poem he had in fact once tried to write, a parody of Marvell that had grown out of reminiscences traded with a pipe-chewing faculty associate, about the beastly cost of almost any sexual hanky-panky, let alone the kind of structured long-term adultery with which both had had some experience. Peckham dug it up, liked the fragments he had ground out well enough to round them out with some fresh couplets, and sent off the result to Binnie and her *Whirligig*. Surely any literate American must be familiar enough with "To His Coy Mistress" to appreciate what was obviously a pastiche of the original in reverse:

TO HIS IMPORTUNATE MISTRESS
(Andrew Marvell Updated)

Had we but world enough, and time,
My coyness, lady, were a crime,
But at my back I always hear
Time's wingèd chariot, striking fear
The hour is nigh when creditors

Will prove to be my predators.
As wages of our picaresque,
Bag lunches bolted at my desk
Must stand as fealty to you
For each expensive rendezvous.
Obeisance at your marble feet
Deserves the best-appointed suite,
And would have, lacked I not the pelf
To pleasure also thus myself;
But aptly sumptuous amorous scenes
Rule out the rake of modest means.

Since mistress presupposes wife,
It means a doubly costly life;
For fools by second passion fired
A second income is required,
The earning which consumes the hours
They'd hoped to spend in rented bowers.
To hostelries the worst of fates
That weekly raise their daily rates!
I gather, lady, from your scoffing
A bloke more solvent in the offing.
So revels thus to rivals go
For want of monetary flow.
How vexing that inconstant cash
The constant suitor must abash,
Who with excuses vainly pled
Must rue the undisheveled bed,
And that for paltry reasons given
His conscience may remain unriven.

The reply he shortly received was from an associate editor of *Whirligig* named Jack Bimberhoff, who wrote: "I'm sorry to say that Binnie Aspenwall is no longer with us, and so I am replying in her stead to say that while we liked and enormously admired the enclosed poem, we feel it a little special for our readers. A parody of Andrew Marvell would be well over the head of most magazine readers anywhere, wouldn't you say. How many would ever have heard of Andrew Marvell, let alone know that he is one of our most important American poets.

"I hope that this will not discourage you from trying us again, because I think you have talent, if it could be profitably channeled. Do you ever write prose? We are planning an early special issue on 'Dress Today,' how people do it and so on, and wonder if you would care to knock out, say, 2000 words for us on the difference between how you dress on weekdays than weekends. In the case of a shirt without necktie, would you leave the neck open one more button lower on weekends, or in the country as against the city, for informality? That sort of thing. If interested do please drop me a line, or even phone me at the above number."

Peckham was still shaking his head, reassured in his conviction that he was surrounded by imbeciles, when he again heard from Binnie, with the same quiver of excitement as in the previous instance. "Ms. Aspenwall" this time appeared on the envelope over the return address of Sherman and Cromley, Theatrical Productions, and the letter was again addressed to him care of Dogwinkle and Dearie, proof that she had left or been fired from *Whirligig* before receiving his response.

"Dear Earl: Guess what! I'm in the theatre! Fact. I have a job in the office of this production company who are planning a revue for next spring, probably Off Broadway but with ultimate removal to Broadway definitely in mind. It's tentatively entitled 'Let's Face It.' We welcome, indeed hunger for, good sketches on any current subject, with particular emphasis on the present sexual mores, the changing attitudes, etc. Do you by any chance have any idea or ideas buzzing about in that fertile noddle of yours that might lend itself to a short stage satire . . .?"

No man not to see a farce played out to its end, Peckham again responded, again easily enough by pulling something out of his trunk. It was a sketch he had batted out for a joint faculty-student revue called *Skimble Skamble,* put on in his last year but one as a college teacher. It had come off pretty well then, and now it struck him as more relevant today than even that short time ago. And "Accommodation" did have that sine qua non for any theatrical sketch, a good blackout line. The piece called for only a Man and a Woman, and ran:

M.C.: We all know about the New Morality as regards sex. In its wake inevitably comes the New Flexibility—the need to be broad-minded, permissive toward each *other's* proclivities when they unexpectedly surface, however quirkily and in forms however unorthodox. Here are two people faced with the need to make precisely that kind of adjustment in the androgynous society toward which they say we are irresistibly swept.

Couple at restaurant table. MAN *fiddling with the condiments on the checkered tablecloth. He's wearing a splashy shirt, she a pinstripe suit with Brooks Brothers button-down shirt and necktie.*

WOMAN: You *know* what Freud said.

MAN: Yeah. If all the repressed women were laid end to end, it'd be a damn good thing, and a better world all around.

WOMAN: He said—ignoring the deliberately churlish vulgarity of the reply—he said, "There are so certainly masculine and feminine elements in every person, I'm convinced that when two people are making love there are four people in bed together." Such is the human makeup.

MAN: Speaking of makeup, I wish you wouldn't use that green stuff on your eyelids. It makes you look like a Key Lime pie. Hon.

WOMAN: So now it's all out in the open. Your hostility. Have you any other criticisms you might wish to ventilate? My breathing habits, perchance, my family?

MAN: Well, now that you mention it, your brother. He's a thorn in my flesh.

WOMAN: Of which, I might observe, there is annually an increasing quantity.

MAN: It's one thing to have a brother-in-law who works only two weeks in the year, if that—

WOMAN: *(Smiling acidly, but to herself, as though in full knowledge of a nuance to be lost on its object)* You have a chronically unemployed brother-in-law hanging around the house. How bromidic.

MAN: Yeah. And speaking of annually increasing quantities of the old poundage, he's going to have to lose twenty even to get Santa Claus work come Yuletide. How does that grab you, a guy who's going to have to slim down to get a job as Santa? That's how fat he's gotten.

WOMAN: I do wish you wouldn't say 'gotten.'

MAN: Why not?

WOMAN: It always grated on Auden.

MAN: W. H.?

WOMAN: That's the one. "That curious American verb 'gotten,' " I heard him say. Right here at this table. Of course I was sitting at the next one, agog at his every word. And damned if he didn't say the same thing one morning on the *Today* show when Barbara Walters was running it. Of course the British say "got." He laughed when he made the remark, but you could tell it grated on him.

MAN: Speaking of grated, did you know the Parmesan cheese they put in these shakers for the spaghetti is grated fresh every day? Hon?

WOMAN: Oh, my God! So am I!

MAN: So are you what?

WOMAN: Grated fresh every day! By your—gaucheries. Do you realize what your conversation runs to? It comes to me just now. Something men normally accuse we women of. Non sequiturs. I've been noticing other such traits in your nature, the evidence mounts.

MAN: Like what?

WOMAN: Have you noticed how you're eternally rearranging the furniture? Shoving the chairs and the tables and the sofa here and there and everywhere.

MAN: To keep them out from under where the goddamn roof leaks! I keep neglecting the repairs around the house you have to keep nagging me about. That's masculine. No doubt about that. I think I can spit over my chin, all right. Huh!

WOMAN: And the way you keep squeezing a tube of toothpaste in the middle—that's supposed to be *our* idiosyncrasy. Men customarily roll it up from the bottom, to keep it round and firm and fully packed. A symbolism it would be too frightfully hackneyed to mention, albeit too cryptic for your comprehension.

MAN: Yeah? Not that word again, not "phallic." Everything these days is phallic.

WOMAN: (*Archly patting her back hair*). Except perhaps the contemporary male instrument.

MAN: Would you care to step outside and repeat that? (*He springs to his feet and genially hams it up, weaving and bobbing, swiping thumb across tongue and making with the dukes.*) How ofttimes we heard that around here, in the old days when it was a saloon, more. "I don't suppose you'd care to step

165

outside and repeat that, Mac." "My name isn't Mac. It's Wilberforce." "Oh, yeah? Well, we ain't got time for all them syllables. Outside, please?" Even with your brother—before I met you, and before he got so fat we're going to have to get off twenty pounds by Christmas to get him another brief stint on Macy's payroll. One time me and him—

WOMAN: *(Ironically)* Him and me would, I think, be the preferred usage.

MAN: Him and me got into a fight when we were strangers and ended up buddies. Went out the door arm-in-arm.

WOMAN: Oh?

MAN: "Let's go out and pick up a couple broads." That was the refrain around here. Ah, those were the days. "Let's go out and pick up a couple broads."

WOMAN: That's what men did together then, eh? Well.

MAN: One day we did, and one of them was you. That's how we met, remember?

WOMAN: And you would like your freedom to do so again. You have it.

MAN: What do you mean?

WOMAN: Sit down. *(He does.)* There's something I must tell you. I've been leading up to it rather circuitously. Now it's epiphany time. Time to lay my cards on the table and

166

tell you what I've learned about myself, and must ask you to face as I've had to. You've met my analyst.

MAN: The lesbian with doubts about her masculinity?

WOMAN: She's left me with no doubts about mine. That I must go with, release, live with, and by, the long-suppressed homoerotic element in myself. I'm gay, Hank.

MAN: Ah.

WOMAN: No, it's a fact.

MAN: *(Emits a long whistle of amazement)* Well, I'm a sonof-abitch.

WOMAN: Does it blow you away, Hank? Does it wash you ashore?

MAN: No, I know all about this New Flexibility. Even the *Reader's Digest* does. This New Age we're entering, this New Man we're supposed to be breeding. The wave of the future. What was it you called it the other night, when I was shoving the love seat around. This New Man we're breeding?

WOMAN: Androgynous.

MAN: Yeah. Switch-hitting. Well, I know it hasn't been all beer and skittles with us lately. I could sense something brewing that didn't smell like coffee. Still, I think we can be civilized about it. Christ, I never thought it would come to that—being civilized. But what is there to do but accommodate. Pick up the pieces and shuffle along. Couples often have to do that even without one of them changing denominations. Companionship—there's always that. So let's make a start on it. *Now!* (*Bangs the table*) There are still lots of things we can do together.

WOMAN: Like what?

MAN: (*Drops a bill on the table to pay the check and rises*) Let's go out and pick up a couple broads!

(BLACKOUT)

Who would say Earl Peckham lacked the common touch, hey? Who could say that now? Lacked the common touch, indeed! Too rarefied for this world, fiddlesticks! "Accommodation" showed he could be as meat-and-potatoes as the next man any day, it was just that the more elevated plane was his natural habitat. He had a broader spectrum than even he himself had fully realized. He sent the sketch off to Binnie instantly. Three weeks later he received a reply from one Jock Sherman:

"Dear Mr. Peckham: Binnie Aspenwall, I regret to say, is no longer with us, and so I myself undertake the pleasant task of telling you how terrific we think your sketch is. It goes right into the revue, which we hope to go into production on next spring, or at least within the year. You know theatre ventures all take time, what with collecting the right materials, finding the right director, raising the money, and a thousand other things. We have a broad net out for sketches, songs and lyrics from the best writers, composers and lyricists, so 'Let's Face It' will take some time to assemble properly. But we have every hope that you will be hearing positive things from us in a very short time. Meanwhile . . ."

The meanwhile stretched into weeks, then months and, as Peckham feared, knowing full well the uncertainties of the theater, years. Meanwhile he had sense enough not to hold his breath till he got a contract (which turned out to be never, as the whole project fizzled out), and meanwhile, too, there were Poppy McCloud's rather more tangible developments to absorb their interests, however interlaced, now, with a persistent curiosity about Binnie and her mysterious comings and goings. He scoured the local telephone books in vain for Hysters and Aspenwalls, then tried to forget about her, though nagged with an intimation that she would turn up again, in one guise or another.

Watching in anguish for Poppy's mail turned out to be needless. One afternoon the phone rang and it was a *New Yorker* editor saying they liked and wanted "Country Chic" and, finding her name in the suburban book, he was taking the liberty of calling her to say so. Liberty! They spun in ecstasy for days. And Peckham imputed it to himself for righteousness that his joy in her joy far outweighed the envy he naturally felt as one who himself had never managed to make the grade with *The New Yorker*. The editor had said he would like to meet her and asked could she join him for lunch at the Algonquin. He wanted to go over one or two minor points anyway.

High noon of the Algonquin day found Peckham sitting

in his study, or what his so far successfully avoided neighbors would no doubt have called his den, another word that made his flesh creep. He preened himself on his self-abnegation, and why not? He was "devoting himself to her career," as the gossip columnists would say in jabbering away about celebrities' wives and husbands. Had he not always been respectful of Poppy, even a gentleman if it came to that? Not too hastily familiar even when things between them were obviously on the boil in jolly old Omaha? In fact it had not been till mid-coitus that he had said "Give us a kiss," if memory served. Now he was willingly playing second fiddle, though of course secretly relishing his role as power behind the throne, in a quasi-diabolical way.

That continued with his suggesting three more sections of the book that might be smelted down into short stories. *The New Yorker* rejected all of them, but took a new one independently written, and their mourning turned again to joy. Also, the three were accepted elsewhere, one by a popular women's periodical, the other two by prestigious new quarterlies—and by that time *The New Yorker* had published "Country Chic," to a flutter of fan mail followed by a letter requesting permission to reprint it in a best-short-stories-of-the-year annual. Then *The New Yorker* bought another, rewritten three times under Peckham's hammering tutelage. Poppy was on her way.

A blue note was sounded by Toedink, the agent, squawking because her stories were not being routed to him for submission. He was reminded that he had no contract with her and told that he would continue to handle only book and subsidiary rights. Next to be heard from was Dogwinkle, through whose burble of congratulations could be detected a hint of alarm that one of his stars had taken a turn for the better.

"When can we expect the new book?" he asked, over the phone.

"Probably next fall."

"Swell. Then we can shoot for a spring publication. And the novel should benefit by the kudos the stories will no doubt have collected. Right on."

He was not so right-onish when the opus was delivered as promised.

"A collection of stories?" His features went slightly gray, ashen even, as though he had envisioned beyond that the specter that haunts all publishers—a volume of poetry. "I figured that— Don't you think that another novel should follow *Dawn*, to consolidate your reputation, so *it* could help us coast for a bit on a collection of stories? We'd have to negotiate a separate contract for that, you know. Present one is only for novels."

It was her stories that had consolidated her reputation, or begun to, in the literary quarters rightly so called, and this with no collection yet. She was talked about at the publication-day parties of other authors and had been treated in two articles on "the new short story" that had appeared in news magazines. Emphasis was laid on the youth of the newcomers and the fact that most of them were women. Their characters were all "unrooted, as distinguished from uprooted," as *Time* put it. They were for the most part sexual migrants, wandering from one impermanent rela-

171

tionship to another, not even hoping for stability. They went from partner to partner, wearing "the shackles of liberation." It wasn't even a case of disenchantment— just unenchantment. They'd never had any illusions to lose. All of her stories illustrated a new kind of sexual realism, except for the two that had been printed in *The New Yorker*, steadfast in its opposition to erotic blatancy. Poppy was definitely part of a new fictional school, if not indeed at the dead center of it. "Dirty romanticism" was a name Peckham privately thought of as possible for it, in case he might be called upon to christen it, but that he kept to himself for the time being.

"How many are there?" Dogwinkle asked, riffling through the paste-up she had delivered by hand to his office.

"Fourteen. Almost the bulk of your average novel."

Peckham eagerly awaited her report at home, where he was fixing beef Stroganoff for their dinner. He had always prepared many of his own meals and was now content to play chief cook and bottle washer as a small price to pay for keeping servants out of their little nest in Gladwyn.

"Dogwinkle figures you're the—what was that expression of W. C. Fields?"

"Nubian in the fuel supply."

"Yes. You're the Nubian in the fuel supply. He hit the ceiling when I told him the stories came from raiding the novel. That's what he wants, of course. Now he thinks that plump roasted turkey has been cut up into wings and drumsticks and slices of white meat and second joints, and all the king's men can't put it together again."

"What did he think of the title?"

"*Rotten Persimmons?* He looked as if he had bitten into

172

one. I told him there was a firm tradition of naming a collection after one of the stories. He said he would go over the other thirteen."

"We'll have that bottle of Margaux with this, so probably nothing before dinner, but maybe a brandy or two after, to get semi-fried on before we hit the sack."

She pitched into her share of his hearty casserole, then midway the dinner turned pensive, sipping her wine with an abstracted air. Where was the perpetual chatter laced with perpetual laughter issuing from lips perpetually fresh? It had dried up, as suddenly it could.

"What?"

"It's the content of what I write. Not the how, that's the result of what you've taught me, in fact you've taught me to write, and I'm eternally grateful. It's the what. The ideas I express, the mood in what I write, that seems like your influence too. I'm not naturally this pessimistic. The optimistic me of ten years ago wouldn't recognize the me of *Rotten Persimmons.*"

"If it's the title that bothers you too, we could go back to the other—*Sordid Details.* That has a nice resonance to it. And you're ten years older than you were ten years ago. You've learned that life is a rained-on parade. Consequently you're using the black keys more. You're minoring your chords."

"Don't try to slip-slide away with one of your clever metaphors. You won't be nailed to the barn door about anything, will you? How does that old Naughty Nineties song go? 'You made me what I am today, I hope you're satisfied.' "

"Wait till you see the reviews of *Rotten* before you complain about *that.* Eat, and drink that wine with a proper reverence for the labor that went into the vineyard. Don't just sip it without tasting it."

" 'Ride a Cock Horse' could have had a happier ending. You've bent me to your will," she said, giving him an affectionate cuff on the chin. "You make me say life stinks, you stinker."

"Haven't our best writers always told us that? Hemingway said it's a bad joke. Fitzgerald called it a fraud. Mark Twain declared it a swindle. Someone else whose name escapes me called it a tale told by an idiot. The best we can have with it is a lover's quarrel, and the poet of that conceit told God he had played a big joke on him. Eliot said 'end of the endless journey to no end.' The world is a cesspool, life stinks, and man is a mistake."

"Wow. Are you sure?"

"Positive."

"How do you know?"

"Because he weaves and is clothed with derision, sows and he shall not reap, his life is a watch or a vision, between a sleep and a sleep. He tills the earth and lies beneath, and after many a summer dies the swan. Eat."

"You threw two poets at me at once there, didn't you. The second was Tennyson, but who was the first?"

"Swinburne. Who's turning over in his grave at the way you don't even bother to savor what you're drinking. This Margaux cost thirty dollars a bottle. At six glasses in a bottle and five good gulps to the glass, that's thirty swallows in a bottle, or a dollar per mouthful. So some respectful attention to each one, please. Be more like me."

"There, you see. Total domination of your victim is

174

what you want. Are you dissatisfied with the way I'm sticking these eats in my mouth too?"

"Well, yes, with the rotation. I mean don't drink the Margaux after a forkful of salad, for God's sake. After the Stroganoff. There you'll have some counterpoint with the wine, especially if, like I say, you breathe slowly through your nose with your mouth closed, to get the 'finish.' Or what a lady I know who never knows what she's saying called the 'boutique.' " What in God's name had brought Mrs. DelBelly to mind? "The bouquet, you know, is principally in the olfactory afterward, not the sniffing and swirling beforehand."

"I suppose as your disciple I should do what you say."

"Of course. Here." He tipped the last of the bottle into her glass, careful not to pour the dregs. She shoved it across to him, taking his empty one. "Here, you drink it. I'll have that brandy instead, after five miles on the bike."

They had an Exercycle in their bedroom, which she used more faithfully than he, what with the weight struggle frequently waged by those who have quit smoking. Peckham took his turns just pedaling along with a book on the handlebars—currently Kafka, whom he was rereading. She watched both the speedometer and the odometer more closely, grimly determined to clock five miles daily at fifty miles an hour. He watched stretched out on the bed, a snifter of Courvoisier balanced on his stomach, as she pumped away at today's heat in her gray gym suit, bent over for all the world like a six-day bike racer. At last she dismounted, puffing heavily as she pulled the suit off. "Whew."

He smiled over. "Like to take a shower?"

"Oh, I'm too dirty and sweaty."

"You could take a bath first, if that's the way you feel about it. I don't mind. Or you could take a quick shower and *then* I could pop in with you. You're so dainty," he said rather accusingly, a mite irked with himself for using an advertising word that set his teeth on edge.

"Oh, I don't feel much like a romp tonight. You wouldn't either after spending the day with Bert Dogwinkle. You mean there's no point in anything, anywhere, anyhow? Why are we here?"

In answer he began lustily to sing a song. "We're here because we're here because we're heeeeeeere. We're here because—"

"Yes, yes, I remember that campfire thing. That was just for nonsense. You mean all the while us kids never dreamed it had teleological implications?"

"There is nothing in the universe worthy of your worship. Bertrand Russell."

"Swell. Soo. I'll just go cut my throat and take a shower and you be a dear and mop up after me, like Anthony Perkins in *Psycho*."

"You don't want to kiss the cook?"

"Oh, all right. Give me five minutes or so and then I'll be receiving."

"If you plan to wash your hair let me do it. I like lathering in the shampoo with my fingers. It's so scooshy and obscene. Reminds me of the scene in *Moby-Dick* where the narrator goes into a kind of rapture *squeezing, squeezing, squeezing* the whale sperm."

As she marched into the bathroom she threw a smile

over her shoulder whose secret content he could not have dreamt. His last words had already mentally gone into one of the principal scenes of a story she was writing. It was about a Memphis girl who gets involved with an educated creep.

The reviews of *Rotten Persimmons and Other Stories* were everything he had told her to expect. "Mordant . . . cut deep and bite hard . . . searing details . . . the unrooted set . . . minimal—take the arc for the full circle . . . a meal of scraps . . . elliptical . . . fragmentariness devisedly aimed at reflecting that of life itself. . ." They echoed the jacket copy Peckham had written for it. The critic for the *Times Book Review* said: "It's hard to believe this came from the pulp author who gave us 'Break Slowly, Dawn.' She must, like Fitzgerald, be able to write with her left and right hand both. He constantly did the former for the slick magazines and their money, as Faulkner quite compliantly did for the movie moguls. 'Wrote two stories,' Scott is reported to have written a friend. 'One good and one lousy.' Ms. McCloud can apparently do likewise, turning on now the one tap, now the other."

The one tap is shut for good, Peckham thought to himself, rubbing his hands as Dogwinkle and Dearie tore their hair. For the royalty statements recorded the precipitate plummet in sales that removed any remaining doubt that here was a writer for the discerning few. She was not for the great unwashed, who came however well bathed and groomed into New York and Chicago and Detroit and Cedar Rapids and Omaha and Denver and Seattle book-

stores, armed with bestseller lists from which to make their
selections. People who—sickening phrase!—"caught up
on their reading." No, she had arrived, and would not
depart while there was breath in him. It would be too
much to say that he had found talent and made it genius.
But he had found ability and made it talent.

He even kept a close eye on her public performances—
for she was asked to read from her works as she never had
from *Break Slowly, Dawn*—going so far as to coach her in
her delivery, her emphases, her gestures as well, and sup-
plying bridging commentary, or "mortar," between one
piece and the next. His self-effacement bordered on the
ostentatious, for there were many who knew that the tall
slender figure sitting or standing unobtrusively at the back
of the auditorium, watching as she scribbled autographs
following a performance, was her live-in, said to be a writer
in his own right. Her audiences swelled as her TV interviews and book-and-author-luncheon appearances in-
creased, and there was an occasion when the turnout at
a New York college overflowed even the standing room
of the hall for which the reading was scheduled, and the
entire audience had to troop across campus to the main
auditorium with its more spacious accommodations. Peckham scurried through it to her side just in time to hand
her a slip of paper on which he had scrawled an opening
quip for use when she finally reached the lectern. "Sorry
about the inconvenience, ladies and gentlemen, but at
least for once I can honestly say that I moved an audience."
Great ice-breaking boffo.

The remodeling job was far from limited to the artistic

sphere. He refined her tastes as well, till at times they gave promise of approximating even his own impeccability in that area. This was done with the most delicate adherence to the standards of private courtesy themselves. When rebuking her for some slip of preference, some booboo of discernment, he would not do so frontally, saying "Pullease!" like a paving contractor bawling out a wife for buying a hat he wouldn't take her to a dog show in. No, he would do so with the obliquity in which he had schooled her as a literary artist. He would tilt an eyebrow or purse his lips in a smile of approval so faint as to constitute unmistakably its reverse. Or when a more marked grade of opposition was indicated, he would lay two fingers on her wrist and say, "My dear," at the same time lowering the Svengali wattage in his eyes below the level at which he fixed her when directly criticizing her work, where no compromise must be allowed. This might be illustrated in simple things like shopping together. Once at Lord & Taylor she spotted a bit of gimcrackery called a funbrella, whose name alone should have made one's blood run cold. It was a tall glass with a small parasol fitted to it that was humorously aimed at shielding its contents from the sun's rays and thus preserving the coolness of one's drink in hot summer weather. "Oh, let's get half a dozen," she said. "They'll be swell for beach picnics, or even on the patio." "My dear." He touched her forearm with a finger. It was enough. It served its kind pedagogical purpose. She lowered her own gaze with an expression of endearing apology. She had again learned, again been raised a notch in sensibility. In the end she was fit for his friends—or would

179

have been if he'd had any. Till he got some, they would have to worry along with hers—and their mutual publisher's "set," and even that of their common agent's. And "common" was good when it came to the latter, that avaricious Dutchman named Toedink who raised louder hell than Dogwinkle over her rise in the literary world and its concomitant nosedive in sales. So steep that they were not getting so much as a smell of the bestseller list. Not one store in all this country had "reported" *Rotten Persimmons*, though it was rumored to be a candidate for some prestigious prize awarded by critics. That should seal its commercial doom!

Dogwinkle invited them all to lunch for a crisis talk.

"Well, Peckham," Dogwinkle began once they were all settled at the Four Seasons, which alone would cost somebody a bundle. "When are we going to get something from you again? Isn't it about time? You *are* with book, I trust."

This was so transparent that Peckham nearly laughed aloud. Dogwinkle wanted Peckham to get the hell back to production on another novel so that he could leave Poppy alone to work free of his influence and, having recovered her shortcomings, turn out another piece of claptrap for the charts. Nevertheless he replied, "I get to the new one once in awhile, when I can."

"Ask the title?"

"Vain Deluding Joys."

"Spot of the old despair again. Mean to say, if you could just give people *something*. They don't ask much. Just a shred of reason for going on."

"I'm sorry, I can't do that," Peckham said, in the tone

180

of a man of unshakable probity, one who cannot be bought off.

"Maybe if you took out the 'vain.' Just *Deluding Hope* would be enough."

"It's *Deluding Joys*. Title is from Milton. Blind chap who wrote some epics. This is from 'Il Penseroso.' 'These pleasures, Melancholy, give, / and I with thee will choose to live.' Thinking of that for an epigraph."

They lapsed into a moody silence, as if adopting the program determined on by the bard. Not that Toedink needed any injunction. He was already sufficiently deep in the dumps at Poppy's ascension to cult status on work he wasn't getting a penny from. He was a Frisian, a strain said to be even more Dutch-stubborn than the rest of the Hollanders in The Netherlands. The others watched him trowel some pâté onto a shard of toast and tuck it between his thin lips. The color of the paste reminded Peckham of the peanut-butter-and-jelly sandwich very possibly still stuck in the shrubbery at Dappled Shade, though worn by now to a scrap of its former self by the rains and snows and beating suns of—how many years since? Three? It seemed like only yesterday and also, of course, like a hundred years ago.

"When are we going to get another buxom book?" Toedink finally asked Poppy. It was a favorite term of his, for a novel of eight hundred pages or more, and weighing five pounds or so, and costing, perforce, nearly twenty dollars. Peckham called them fat slobs, these books.

"She's writing poetry," he said.

An involuntary cry of pain was torn from Toedink,

181

while Dogwinkle went the usual ashen gray he turned on receipt of publishing information of a ghoulish nature.

"He's just teasing you," Poppy said, as one might tell an Inquisition victim on the rack that his papal tormentors were just teasing him. "I'll get around to a novel soon. But meanwhile why don't you rejoice in the reviews I've got for the stories? Did you read the piece about the Vagabonds in the *Village Voice*?"

That was more of Peckham's behind-the-scenes work. He had decided against "The Dirty Romantics" as a name for the group of writers with whom Poppy was now firmly associated, in favor of "The Vagabonds," which would emphasize the fact that their characters were all sexual itinerants wandering from one ephemeral relationship to another. He had even timed its first public use. She would spring it in a television interview for which she was scheduled on PBS. It had caught on instantly, and here they were discussing the piece in the *Village Voice* about the Vagabond school. Or at least Poppy and Peckham were. Neither Toedink nor Dogwinkle had read it, though the latter had it on his desk for early perusal.

Poppy soon tired of this business talk, distracting herself by looking around the restaurant for celebrities. One was a fashion designer, and he was seated at a nearby table ogling *her*. The chic Italian rose and strolled over with a copy of her book to sign, if she would. She did so, with a pen he himself provided, beaming with pleasure as she returned it to him. Peckham couldn't make out the inscription, but he thought he caught the word "admiration" in it. The man bowed from a waist impeccably sheathed in one of his own jackets and withdrew in a luscious exchange of smiles that suggested a mutual-admiration society from which anything might develop between any two such pretty people. Toedink and Dogwinkle responded with pallid versions of the Latin's luscious grin, and then the men raised their glasses of white wine to her, Toedink doing so after ritualistically sniffing it with his Seckel-pear nose. But Peckham knew that in their heart of hearts they were secretly telling him to eat his own out; it was what he got for playing God, being put in the shade by his own creation. Peckham was too human not to be wincing inwardly at his exclusion, but he certainly didn't show it to them. Knowing that Dogwinkle and Dearie had lost two other commercial mainstays, these through migration to rival publishers, and that the firm was hurting and rumored to be a takeover candidate as the only means of saving its skin, he knew also that Dogwinkle was waiting to reject Peckham's new effort as unmarketable for reasons of literary excellence. That was exactly what happened. "As I've told you and you already knew, popular authors have always subsidized your kind. We couldn't bring you out without them. Now you've lost your meal ticket." But all that lay in the future, one of Poppy's "flashforwards." Dogwinkle had not quite yet hung him out to dry.

Choking back his envy was no big deal for our Peckham, and there was more to it than the compensatory gratifications of playing Svengali. When in her innocence of the real truth Poppy persisted in thinking of their relationship as that the Henry Higgins–Eliza Doolittle less

183

demonic kind, Peckham reminded her of the central element in the Pygmalion myth that she had forgotten, like most people. It was Aphrodite who brought Galatea to life, that the sculptor might fall in love with her. Peckham was similarly enamored. And chief among the satisfactions he took in their bond was the absence of any rivalry between them, especially that which was supposedly inevitable among artists, corrosively eating their guts away under felicitously maintained surfaces. He did not envy Poppy McCloud her vogue, which netted her street recognitions, especially down in the Village, nor did she resent him as the mentor to whom she was indebted for it all. Her creator no less. And this in a day when the sex war was deemed to have blazed up into a conflagration now out of control. He smiled at how flabbergasted her friends must be at this union devoid of any of the acids gnawing away at even normal marriages. This for both the militant feminists and the currently counterattacking males, openly fed to the teeth with female bellicosity—battle-axes without husbands! It must beat them to see their household flourish, going from strength to strength against all obstacles. Poppy with her growing celebrity sanctified by sinking sales, he plugging along in her shade and for the time being at least perfectly content to be playing second fiddle. Some must think him a masochist inwardly relishing a pervert's pain at being ever more abysmally overshadowed, outpaced and outshone in the world's eyes. Deriving some kinky gratification at stepping unobtrusively aside when Poppy was accosted on the street for her autograph, as she often was and he often did. He could hear them: "Some people get their hacks out of cringing, you know. Screwy lot. The ultimate in weirdos." "Yeah, he's the living end." "Lot of them don't need whips, you see. They get off on humiliations. They eat shame." "Whores get that a lot. Johns who can't cut it till they're ordered to do something, like mop the floor, or have the hooker dress up in a police uniform, makes her the symbol of authority." "And of course," you could hear the other authority saying, "Sometimes they're sadomasochist. Like to give pain and take it both."

Peckham smiled at his immunity from even the mildest of such strictures one afternoon when, returning from an hour's subordinate-role shopping at the supermarket, he tooled into the driveway in a mood of self-congratulation at the stability and composure of the household he had helped make. It was with a high heart that he lifted his two sacks of groceries out of the Mercedes convertible and carted them through the back door into the kitchen like a delivery boy. There he heard dim sounds coming from overhead, muffled by distance, two floors in fact, but clear enough in character and timbre to suggest their being made with some vehemence. He stole up a flight of stairs to the bedroom landing and stood listening. They continued, louder now, and clearly made by objects being thrown by somebody. They came from the floor above, Poppy's attic study. A paperweight flung against a wall, perhaps, then a metallic racket, unmistakably that of a wastebasket hurled across the floor. He ascended another half-flight of stairs and put his head through the open trapdoor by which the garret was accessible. He could see her past the rim of the wastebasket, which had rolled to the edge of the aperture before coming to a stop. She was sitting at her desk, breathing fire, or emitting smoke from her nostrils in a way that made it seem the case. Her eyes were clearly ablaze.

"So. My stuff is trash."

Then it had happened at last. Emboldened by the glowing reviews of *Rotten Persimmons*, she had found the courage to read the hitherto shunned notices of its predecessor. Piles of clippings lay on the desk before her, including of course the fatal interview which he had known all along would some day catch up with them. She snatched it up and waved it in his face, or as nearly as that could be done across a distance of twenty feet and with his face barely visible to her in the hatchway. She did it simultaneously with taking a healthy drag on the cigarette in the other hand. So he had done it again: driven her back to nicotine with a pithily expressed opinion. He mounted the last three steps like a man completing the ascent of Everest, and having made it, straightened laboriously up, like someone giving a slow-motion picture of the development of primate preman to the posture of Homo sapiens.

"That was as of then."

"How could you bear to take a woman out to dinner of whose work you thought no more than that. Were you sort of slumming, back then in Omaha?"

"It was taken out of context."

"Context schmontext!" Dear God in heaven, was there to be no deliverance from that grating locution? "And what difference does the context make? A word is a word. A judgment is a judgment."

"It was no harsher than your own on yourself. You've used words as bad. My stuff, you said, the truck I write, even my crud, once. I remember your saying that distinctly. I mean I distinctly remember your saying that."

"That's different. That's someone talking about himself. False modesty and so on. It's not like somebody else's put-down."

"But put it in perspective," Peckham said, his mouth dry as parchment and his tongue working its way through what must be the absolute and irreducible last of Dog-winkle's peanut butter. "To recapitulate briefly, I read your work with the greatest of interest and told you, good as it was, it wasn't a patch on what you could do. What you'd done was the ore from which your true gold might be panned. Or to use my other metaphor, I said, 'You're a bird that has been running along the ground. You must now take flight.' "

"Don't worry, I will. Or you will."

There was a peal of silence, during which they both took in the implication of what she had said. Peckham at last found some words, for whatever they were worth as claim for his mentorship.

"You've come very far. And you'll go farther."

"No, you will." She snorted another lungful of smoke. "And include me out on the bouillabaisse, or whatever it was you said you were going to fix. I plan to make a prior engagement."

He stood there uncertainly, his arms hanging at his sides, his posture sagging back to that of prehuman primate.

"Put you under hypnosis again, sweets? Might be best.

Worked the last time—till now. Can't fall off the 'baccy wagon, you know."

A box of paper clips flew across the room in a spray that covered half the floor. Peckham knelt to gather them up and put them back into the cardboard receptacle, with a patient deliberation that fell short of its punitive purpose. He realized that crawling about on all fours in this martyred ministration was totally out of key with their established relationship. He was abdicating his mastership and in so doing was untrue to his charge as well. He climbed to his feet and straightened to his full height. By that time she had herself risen, crushed the butt in an ashtray, and started out of the study. Narrowing his eyes in a current of command that should have been felt clear through her, he said, "Stop this tantrum and get back to work."

"Go milk a yak."

"I will no such thing. *Get back to work.* You've promises to keep. I order it."

"Order a pizza. You'll get it faster."

"Come here."

He'd had to move back a step to make room as she marched past him and down the stairs, which were so steep, little more than a ladder really, that he always went down them backward, as he did following her now, marveling, as ever, at the ease with which she descended them normally. She went on into the bedroom, and standing uncertainly in the corridor just outside it, wondering how he might best rally his forces, he presently heard a rhythmic squeak that indicated she was aboard the Exercycle. A brief reprieve, in any case. Time to rethink his position.

Stealing tentatively into the doorway, he saw that she was again riding hell-for-leather, bent over the handlebars with such graphic verisimilitude as to convey the illusion that she was actually riding a bicycle. Fleeing him as fast as she could, certainly. That was the symbolic implication, so vividly inescapable that he forged a brief counterfantasy of his own. He was chasing her up Fifth Avenue past all the major bookstores, Scribner's, Barnes & Noble, B. Dalton, Doubleday Fifty-third, Doubleday Fifty-sixth, endowed with the foot-speed of the silent-movie comics, but even so hopelessly outpedaled by her, falling farther and farther back till he saw her vanish round the corner at Central Park South where his periodontist was located. If this were a real dream, a customer emerging from the second Doubleday would have come up to him and said, "I read your last book. I found it pedestrian." He crucified himself a little with that and went downstairs, knowing Poppy would do more than her customary five miles this day. She would do at least ten.

"Let her get it out of her system," he said to himself as he set about fixing the bouillabaisse. But she proved as good as her word. She damn well *did* make a prior engagement, backing out of the driveway and zipping off in the Mercedes in a scherzo of departure as he was setting the pot of sea stew on the table. He force-fed himself a dish of it, with some chardonnay that needed considerably less urging. He polished off the whole of the bottle intended for the both of them, so that by the time he dropped into bed, about eleven, he had less trouble falling asleep than he had feared. By then he had nourished into existence the conviction that he was being wronged at least as much as he had done wrong, if not more, and would have said, "Women take everything personally," if doing so would not have flung him into the Gehenna teeming with the mouthers of bromides, like the dismal hubbies who said, "Can't live with 'em, can't live without 'em." It remained for Poppy to sink them hopelessly in marital cliché by returning around eleven and nesting down on the living room sofa. "This is a sitcom," he groaned to himself as he dropped off to sleep, chewing a corner of the pillow at the memory of how one of her autograph hounds had called him Mr. Pullman.

He awoke feeling as though his head had been used as a demolition ball by a wrecking crew, and not at all sure he hadn't actually dreamt something to that effect. But absolutely intact in his head were plans for dealing with their crisis that he had hatched the night before, in fact as early as midway the bottle of chardonnay.

As a veteran of two marriages (or two domestic relationships so close to marriage as made no matter) he was quite familiar with how these pitched battles went, or could be made to go if you waged them right. It was simple. If you said something cutting, you egged your victim on to say something even more cutting, thus turning the tables by making yourself the wronged party. She had already dealt him an advantage by walking out on his swell dinner and huffing off to a rendezvous with which she had compounded her offense by leaving him in the dark about it. But it was not enough of an advantage, not by a long chalk. She must be lured into a far graver felony, and that required the utmost craft. To wind up blameless as a dove, he must be wise as a serpent. She must be maneuvered into dealing him a blow more mortal than he had her, if mortality can be regarded as having degrees. Of course that meant reviving hostilities. And the really effective execution of all this calls for the true connoisseur of pain.

When she robe-and-slippered into the kitchen the next morning, about a quarter to eleven, he was hunched over a bowl of wet reptile scales, more commonly known as cornflakes and milk, engrossed in the printed matter on the package from which he had shaken the former.

"I have always found cereal boxes a good read," he said. "No wasted words, come right to the point. And the resonance of the enumerated vitamins is without comparison. Listen to this and say honestly whether a passage in Tennyson at his most bombastic can match it for sheer phonetic power. 'Thiamin, riboflavin—' Pause over that one, roll it on the tongue. 'Ri-bo-flavin.' Has more flavor than the stuff itself. Then there's—"

"I'm sorry about yesterday. I guess I overreacted."

What? What's this? No, this will not do. We can't both be let off the hook with a simple little twist of apology. We must go on to our appointed bloodbath. That you must try that easy exit from the labyrinth we've entered with your back turned at the stove shows you yourself are ashamed of the attempted copout. We have a respectable *comédie noire* within our grasp—everything I've taught you as the inescapable sine qua non of our common human muddle and that you finally embodied in your work—and now you want to drag us back down to sitcom? Namby-pamby Handy-Andy eight-o'clock prime-time I'm-sorry-I-hurt-you-darling television pap? No, oho no, we cannot backslide into that. We must go on to the end, a hard-won but creditable resolution to a comedy than which nothing could be more *noir*. Nothing less than honest lacerations will do, one another's entrails strewn across the linoleum floor in an obligatory scene worthy of the name and unflinchingly true to dramatic ingredients inherent in our fortuitous meeting from the first—if not from the fatal foundations of the world. Our ecstatic but misbegotten edifice will not be brought down in a cheap heap by a paltry twinge of remorse conveyed in that trite merry-marital-mixup of a word, *overreacted*. That's for the amateurs, not the pros. This is not a tempest in a teapot. This is a teapot in a tempest, and somebody's got to be cracked on the noggin with it, if not hard enough for a skull fracture then at least a nasty little concussion.

"Then you admit I was right?"

"How, right? In what you said?"

"Mmm, yes."

"I mean, to the reporter?"

"Well, yes. That's what you're talking about, isn't it? What we're talking about?"

"And you stood in that bookstore in Omaha with your bare face hanging out, telling me how much you enjoyed it."

"What else could I say after your compliment to me? And there were parts in *Dawn* I could honestly say I thought not too—"

"Isn't this a little weasely?"

"If that's the name you want to give common human courtesy, yes."

Water was poured into a pan and the pan was clapped down on the stove with a force that indicated hostilities had been successfully reopened.

"Common courtesy, swell. The fact of the matter was that I may have been a little more lavish in my compliments about *Sorry Scheme* than the facts warranted. Two can play at the courtesy game, you know."

"Aha! Now it's out."

Peckham had read somewhere, years before, that evidence of male and female token possession of one another's hormonal components lay in the way each one's voice changed in the course of an argument. Women lowered theirs in a way that somehow gave more lethal force to their barbs, while in the heat of a dispute a man's tended to go up. He noted now how Poppy spoke in that almost basslike pitch as she returned thrust for parry, parry for thrust, and doing so, he made a conscious effort to keep out of the upper registers himself. Determined not to fall into the soprano range—if "fall" is the right description of such an admittedly stigmatizing shift—he held his end up in the most throaty tones—just like a woman. (Well, hell, there was no way out of this rap. The explainers overrunning the twentieth century gotcha coming and they gotcha going. Damned if you did and damned if you didn't.)

"How was your previous engagement?"

"None of your beeswax."

"That much of a bummer, eh? Anybody you know?"

"This loopy arcane stuff does get on the nerves. I don't think you know what that means yourself, except that in some esoteric way it's supposed to be snide. It's in your books too. Those hemisemidemiquavers. That was the one aspect I didn't like, but I didn't call it angel's hair, or whatever the counterpart of trash is, and I didn't babble to reporters or television hosts."

Angel's hair. They were cutting close to the bone now. Indeed, it may have been the knife thrust into which he had all the while been trying to lure her. There remained only to make her twist the knife in the wound.

"I notice your moving closer in the direction of subtlety did it for you. Not that you haven't still a little distance to go, my dear. Don't try to hold up your end by scoring off me. At least I don't say 'fevered brow' and 'increasing awareness' and 'groaning board.' "

"And I don't go in for—eyebrow combing!"

That did it. That was it, the twist of the knife from which she would herself recoil in regret far keener than the pain under which he would reel. His lips writhed in a grimace as he took in the gasp of remorse with which she heard what she had said, uttered all but simultaneously with the saying. The advantage was irreversibly his now. The gory game had been won. He could pick up all the marbles.

III

NINE

Among Poppy McCloud's devices that Peckham had eventually got around to accepting and even fancying was the flashforward. It has a tradition hardly conspicuous but certainly respectable, as does the novelistic device of even shuttling incessantly among past, present and future. Little wonder then that we see him back at Dappled Shade with lots more still to relate as to what landed him back there again and why.

He is sitting under what had in the first instance become his favorite tree, a great spreading sycamore, whose scruffy bark often appeals to skewed or melancholy natures, as far as possible from, say, the obvious poetry of the willow, frequently encountered on riverbanks that abet a scene such as might have been painted by a resourceless painter circa 1820. On his lap is a copy of his new novel, *The Ghastly Dinner Party*, an unsparing delineation of the worm-eaten psyche of modern man as exemplified in the sub-cutaneous motivations propelling the social lives of urban people whose surfaces are rotten enough. A first printing of four hundred has been half exhausted in the form of review copies necessarily sent out by the publisher, a southern university press. The notices have been mixed, that is, not nearly as bad as those that greeted *Moby-Dick* when it was first issued. Certainly at odds with them is the handsome jacket blurb supplied by Poppy McCloud, immediately on receipt of the bound galleys. "I know of no novelist today so skillful at grasping both the pleasures and the tensions of the sexual relations of contemporary people, both in the bedroom and out." He rereads it with renewed gratitude. It should go far toward taking the curse off any reviews read by the browser, which is almost certain to be none in any case, particularly in cities like Cedar Rapids and Omaha where the heart of true humanity beats. People in droves must not even have seen the Sunday *Times Book Review*, where fortunately buried on a back page was a review that ran in part: "Earl Peckham strives to be 'searing,' and often is, in his accounts of marital relations, such as the scene in which the wife drops strands of sausage casing into her slumbering husband's open mouth, in an almost emotionally anesthetized curiosity as to how many it will take to choke him to death. Other episodes are less lyrically rendered. What strikes the reader, though, is how derivative of the Vagabond School the work is. He is obviously under its spell, clearly influenced by Poppy McCloud, Genevieve Flappington and Pui Po . . . ."

He had walked his Village apartment for an hour after reading that, swiveling a fist in a palm as an apothecary would a pestle in a mortar, murmuring to himself, "Influence . . . derivative . . . spell . . . reminiscent of . . . I created that school, even gave it its name, for Christ's

sake, and now I'm influenced by it? What the hell is this?"
The suspicion that he might now at long last be going
round the bend was not engendered, exactly, by the way
he tore out page after page of that issue of the *Book Review*,
deliberately, one at a time, wadded it up into the shape
and size of a baseball, and hurled it against the wall so
that it would drop into a wastebasket placed there to
receive it. Lots of people do that. It was not even the way
he sometimes pitched from a stretch. No. It was the way
he looked toward first and third each time before throwing.

But fears had been groundless. If quirky turns of behavior
and odd idiosyncrasies made us committable, we should
none of us be on the outside. They often as not, on the
contrary, keep us sane. And a mixed press—or mixed-up
press, as he liked to think of it—could hardly send Peckham back to Dappled Shade. He wasn't here as a patient
anyway, this time. He was here as a visitor, waiting under
the sycamore for his ailing acquaintance to show up. Which
calls for another of the time shifts dear to latter-day nov-
elists, especially the good old avant-garde, always limping
along in the train of things, the very caboose of literature.

For a flashback—now, try to get this on one go-around—
for a flashback within a flashback *itself enveloped in a flashforward*, we return to the little nest in Gladwyn in the
days immediately following the kitchen slaughter there.
Poppy's and Earl's fair share of the sex war might have
been considered a standoff, and in a sense it was. Yet in
a larger sense (as Abraham Lincoln might have put it) it
was a double knockout, though Peckham still thought and
still thinks he got the better of the battle by being the

more severely battered to a pulp. And that not merely as a card-carrying sadomasochist. "Oh, my God," Poppy'd cried, sinking onto a chair and putting her head in her hand. "What have I said. That was an unkind cut."

"The unkindest cut of all. But it's over and done with. Forget it" had been his memorable reply.

"To go that far just to accuse you of being, well, somewhat overfastidious. Your prose is excessively superb, you know."

"Show me no mercy." Parting the lapels of his bathrobe to offer his heart for the plucking. Let ravens eat it, eagles drive their beaks into it. Quite unlike the time he had extended it in cupped hands to the fleeing Mrs. DelBelly in white moonlight on the gravel walk not far from the very sycamore under which we find him in near tranquillity recollecting that scene in the slaughterhouse kitchen.

"Worked over till every qualifying clause contributes exquisitely to the rhythmic syntax," Poppy dithered on.

"Right, right, I admit it. Say on."

"—like every hair in place, not a hair out of place. Impeccably groomed style—"

"Touché!"

"Till one is, I mean there is such a thing as a surfeit of perfection."

"I know, I know."

"But to put it down with a term like—like I said. I can hardly say it again."

"Try."

"No."

"Yes. It's the only way. Spare neither of us anything.

200

The wound inflicted must be cauterized by the same knife heated. Only then can we both be shriven."

"Not till I've had my coffee."

"All right. I could use a second cup myself."

She had risen, skirted the table, and put her arms around his neck, on the very verge of tears. "That awful damning term. Such a put-down. Eyebrow combing. Oh!"

"There, there. You didn't do it on purpose. We all say things we don't mean," he'd said, wallowing in a voluptuous forgiveness, "not really . . . Let's go upstairs to bed and try to forget about it."

Once, in emphasizing how a flat sentence or phrase can sometimes do more than a polished turn of language in producing a certain impact on a reader, he had read (as often to his students) a passage from Katherine Anne Porter's story "Flowering Judas" to illustrate his point. There is a poignant passage relating how the deeply troubled Laura, born a Roman Catholic, "slips now and again into some crumbling little church, kneels on the chilly stone, and says a Hail Mary on the gold rosary she bought in Tehuantepec." Then the plain words "It is no good." At least as piercing as, if not more so than, the rhythmic swells of fine writing on whose surrounding surfaces it bobs, like a stick on breaking blue sea swells.

They thrashed about in bed, in those heaves of passion with which we sometimes try to generate tenderness, each one's breath a tempest in the other's ear.

"Oh, it's marvelous. This again."

"And this."

"And with my."

"And this way too."

"It's all too. The whole animal is beautiful."

It was no good. Something had happened not any gymnastics could dispel. It was as if—to commit that abhorrent locution he had enjoined all his students to shun as a plague—it was as if a portcullis had dropped between them with a reverberating clang, a hindrance through whose bars they might speak, dine, and even mate, but ultimately as impassable as the padlocked iron gates of Manderley itself. A crowd was hurrying toward it, in hopes that the rain would extinguish the fire threatening to consume it, or perhaps the unworthy human hope that it wouldn't, and they be granted their scene. The multitude of people were divided not spatially, but by the fact that the rain fell on some but not others. In his troubled sleep he struggled to decipher the oddity. If it wasn't falling on the just and the unjust alike, then just who were the just? Scripture itself gave no clue as to the ambiguity. If, as supposed, the just were getting soaked equally with the unjust, then where was the justice in that? Or must rain itself be taken as a life-giving blessing, however discommoding to human beings who were its beneficiaries? He was awakened by Poppy shaking him by the shoulder. "Good God, wake up. You were screaming something terrible. What were you dreaming?"

"I don't remember. Water, fire, air. The elements, I guess. Sorry. Go back to sleep. Will the weevil delay?"

"Don't start that again."

He saw from the phosphorescent hands of their bureau clock that it was 3:10. Why did he always get his worst bucket of buzzard guts in what was billed by the bard as "the first sweet sleep of night"? There was a laugh. How did the Shelley go again? "I arise from dreams of thee / In the first sweet sleep of night, / When the winds are breathing low, / And the stars are shining bright." But then according to the poem's title it was an Indian doing the serenading, not a chewed-up Anglo-Saxon urbanite, with two windows to do the serenading under. Of course he must soon lose this little snuggery in Gladwyn, it was he who must leave it when the impending breakup came and return to what up to now had been the pied-à-terre of their fading idyll, his Village digs. In the customary wakeful pause between his two main periods of sleep, he lay there planning some despair, and then some resurrection to follow. A little *Tod*, a little *Verklärung*. Wasn't that how it had always been, no matter who the partner or whatever the job of work? The stoically accepted tidal rhythm of his life, the seemingly appointed ebb and flow of his luck. Oh, she wouldn't "send him packing." She wasn't that kind. They would simply simultaneously see— had indeed already seen—that the thing had come to its end, and it was time to part. They might even "phase one another out" gradually, each alternately using now the house, now the apartment, as their city-country needs required. Little by little he would take his clothes back to New York, and she likewise eventually cart back to her house what still hung in the Village closet, so pleasantly mixed up with his. One of his former quasi-wives had once said, "I find an affair lasts about three years." All three affairs of his had been good for just about that, give or take a six-month here and there. Where are you now, Cicely? Where are you now, Bernadette? Where are you now, Poppy, for all of that, deep in your own slumbrous adventures here beside me? No, my dears all, the weevil will not delay . . .

That was just about how it went, but Peckham had a long stretch of solitary occupancy in the cottage in Gladwyn as he plugged away hard at his novel, and some other things destined to befall him befell. Work kept him less troubled than might otherwise have been the case at the suspicion that Poppy was as busy in the apartment with amorous engagements as she was with reading ones at such places as the 92nd Street Y. *The Ghastly Dinner Party* was a lot mellower in spots than the bulk of the reviews let on. Such as the opening:

"Cyril Tushingham's contempt for the masses was not total. Many must be given credit for not actually reading the bestsellers they bought, or at least not finishing them. One constantly heard people say of some five-pound quarter-of-a-million-word romance or adventure intrigue, 'I've got through this much of it' or 'I only managed to read so far,' holding up a hand with thumb and forefinger an inch apart, or half an inch. It was no mystery that every season produced what publishers themselves called 'the most widely unread bestseller in the country.' It spoke well for the purchaser that he came to realize he had wasted his money . . ."

Peckham got stuck in a section of the book in which he was dealing with an alcoholic, something with which he had little or no personal familiarity. So one evening he put on his hat and attended what he understood to be an open meeting of Alcoholics Anonymous, held in an upper room of Gladwyn's Congregational church. The session was already in progress, but he was able to make unobtrusively for a free folding chair at the back of the rough circle in which the participants sat, listening to a tall thin man make some sort of testimonial.

"I thought I could taper off, I mean level off, become a moderate drinker. You know—cut down so you don't have to quit? No soap. I had to quit. I could take a drink or two, say, after a couple of weeks, and let it go at that. But a fuse would be lit that would burn slowly inside me, until a few weeks later I'd take another, then another, and find myself on a three-day binge. No, you have to go cold turkey if you're an alcoholic. Become an entirely different person. You have to be—I don't shy at the expression—born again. Like the Christian converts say they are. As Cagney said in that movie where he played a drunk. 'An alcoholic can't lose. If you're down you need a drink, if you're up it calls for one,' or however the speech goes. I can't remember it exactly. Of course he was being ironic . . ."

Peckham's eye began wandering from face to face, most of them in profile from where he sat, trying to make himself as invisible as possible while doing so. Suddenly it was caught by someone he thought he knew—swore he knew—but couldn't place. A woman whose precise identity kept eluding him the instant he felt it on the brink of recognition. Something about the tilt of the chin, the depth of the eye sockets, discernible even from the side, the whorls of blond hair. When the man finished she raised her hand and was recognized by the chairman, or someone serving that function for the evening. The previous speaker had been on his feet, but she began to talk without rising. Peckham's heart popped. It was Binnie . . . Binnie . . . What the devil was her last name again? Mrs. DelBelly's niece. Binnie Aspenwall. Now presumably Mrs. Dempster Hyster. Of certainly bibulous memory, beginning with the housewarming and continuing on through their few fruitless dates. He remembered with a twinge how he had said to her, "If you don't stop drinking you'll become an alcoholic." How idiotic his preachment sounded in memory. It was like telling someone that if he doesn't get some sleep he'll become an insomniac.

"The worst pain an alcoholic must endure is not the misery to himself but the suffering he causes others," she said. "You all know that a kindred organization of this is Al-Anon. Family members, loved ones, who band together to give each other help in dealing with *us* just as we must cope with booze. Well, every Sunday morning you'll find my husband at the chapter meeting at Dappled Shade, giving and taking advice, support and, God knows, commiseration with people having to put up with the likes of us. They have the same prayer as we, that familiar Serenity Prayer. 'God grant me the serenity to accept the things I cannot change, courage to change the things I can, and wisdom to know the difference.' One of the things my husband could change was, he threw me out of the house . . ."

Peckham had lowered his head when she turned her face in his direction, and now he put his fingers in his ears, wishing he might drop through the floor. Flight was impossible, at least for the moment; he could hardly duck out the door without being noticed. Nothing to do but sweat it out. When he unstopped his ears despite himself, keeping his head lowered with one hand shielding his face, she was saying:

"Maybe some of you have been thrown out. It sounds merciless, but we all know it's the only thing to do in some cases. A doctor may advise it, a psychiatrist, we AA members ourselves, when someone refuses to stop or can't stop. The only place for an alcoholic to go up from is absolute rock-bottom. Fathers take the advice and with tears in their eyes throw sons out, daughters even, wives throw husbands out, and vice versa. I went to one meeting of Al-Anon myself, sneaked in without my husband seeing me, and the session had to do with anger. Not much serenity there." Her fellow communicants laughed, and Peckham remembered a line from a poem of Hart Crane's. "With such a sound of gently pitying laughter." His guts turned over inside him, yet there was no escaping the sense of good will pervading this meeting—even good spirits. "Three people testified to throwing family members out of the house, until they could swear off the bottle. What if they have no place to go? That's their problem. What if they turn up again? Call the police. On what complaint? Trespassing. The cruelest way is the only kind one . . ."

When she shifted her eyes in his direction again he

happened to be peeking through his fingers, long enough to know that he had snagged her attention. Had she recognized him? He doubted it. But after she sat down, he noticed that she shifted her chair just a little so as to keep him in her line of vision. Her curiosity had clearly been piqued. Escape was now impossible. He was trapped for the rest of the meeting, which broke up half an hour or so later, after a good deal more from others about serenity. It was apparently a major ideal among alcoholics and their victims both. Peckham had thought serenity something we relinquished at birth and recovered at death, but unobtainable in between. No matter.

With the shuffle of adjournment she drew on a red coat and came right over.

"The Earl of Peckham."

"Hello, Binnie."

"Are you a member of the club?"

"Yes," he said, and instantly realized the lie was regrettable. "Well, no, not really. How about a cup of coffee?"

"Swell. There's a pot here, but that's not what you mean. There's a restaurant down the street where we can go. My car's parked practically in front of it."

As they strolled toward it, she looped an arm through his. After a few minutes of silence, she answered a question naturally on his mind, but which consideration prevented his asking.

"While we've got me on the chopping block, yes, I got fired from those two jobs I had when I wrote you, for reasons easy to guess. Did you submit something when I asked you?"

"Yes, both times. I sent you a poem which somebody whose name I can't remember said was too special for *Whirligig*. Reassuring, after seeing a couple of copies of the magazine. Those theatrical producers were crazy about a sketch I sent *them*, but I see no sign of the revue ever being produced. But I appreciated your asking."

Over coffee he confessed his real purpose in attending the meeting, and Binnie her exaggeration in saying she had been thrown out of the house. Dempster had actually walked out, a chivalrous alternative which came to the same thing—she was left alone. Expelled from his life unless and until she got hold of herself and stayed on the wagon. "I thought it was more, you know, graphic the way I put it, and anyway it's six of one and half a dozen of the other. But tell me about yourself. I think, have to admit to myself, that it was more Aunt Nelly's threatening to disinherit me if I didn't quit drinking, than Dempster's walking out. We were hanging by a thread anyway. The fact of the matter is, it's just as bad living with a workaholic. But you're not telling me about yourself."

"The night I first met you, when we were both scarfing up the chicken paprika like no tomorrow, I seem to remember your saying Tante Nelly would disinherit you if you didn't stop *eating*. You certainly look in good shape now."

"You're sweet. I admit I'm mercenary, as aren't we all. Remember that scene in *Cat on a Hot Tin Roof* where the wife tells her drunken husband how important it is to make sure they get the old man's inheritance. She says something like 'You can be young without money but you can't

209

be old without it.' " Binnie laughed. "I guess I'm saving up for when I'll be old. Saving my aunt's money." Her laugh turned to a sly smile, and she looked at him askance, as though she were planning to deal him a half-share in any mercenary blame. She restrained herself with a generalization. "Lots of men have lusted after it. The money."

"Not to pick up on your implication, she married Dr. Hushnecker, didn't she?"

"Hell no! He couldn't wait till the wedding night. She caught him embezzling funds at the sanitarium, and *pow*. Right out on his ear. I'd like another cup of coffee, it's good here. How about you? Waiter, keep 'em coming."

She seemed to be getting high on caffeine, as was Peckham himself after a second cup. She tapped him playfully on the nose with her spoon and said, "Are you a womanizer?"

"Are you a manizer?"

"There's no such word."

"Why shouldn't there be? Fair's fair. The reality's there."

"For the lady we say, 'She sleeps around.' "

"Hardly more gallant. I suppose there's a note of feminine victimization in the word womanizer, which the feminist would point out. She's a sex object, and so on. But it is odd there's no counterpart word. Unless I just coined it in the cause of equality."

"You still work your mouth pretty good. But I suppose you're right. Woman as a plaything sort of thing, that's the idea behind *womanizer*."

"So your aunt gave Hushnecker the heave-ho. Frankly I could never see him pitching woo—to contribute another to that collection of vintage slang we were getting up, remember? I always sort of thought it 'our' shtick."

"Why do you want to marry my aunt?"

"I'm through with women. To love them is to know them, whereby hangs too many a tale." He thought being facetious, even a little silly, on the subject was the best way to get rid of it. But she wasn't letting him off the hook.

"Doesn't that no-doubt epigram apply to men as well? That to love them is to know them—probably all too well?"

"That goes without saying."

"Then say it." She tapped him on the nose again, as though it were an eggshell that had failed to crack the first time. It hurt just a little. "Do you want to go to my place or your place?"

She had quizzed him enough about his present circumstances to know the question made practical sense. Each lived alone.

He said, "It wouldn't be right. When we saw each other three or four years ago I couldn't take advantage of a wobbly engagement. Now it would be as cheesy-sleazy to do so with a rickety marriage. A man isn't a vulture."

Her lips twisted in a taut smile, and there was an unpleasant flare to her nostrils. He never knew whether she was telling the truth, or reacting with a touch of the woman scorned, when she answered: "What I was asking was whether *you* were *hoping* the evening would end like that, not making the advance. Gawd. Don't make me need a drink."

"Of course. Now that I remember your exact inflection. I guess you wouldn't put it past me at that," he said, to help her save face. "Human nature is after all pretty shabby stuff, take it all in all. But if you were free and clear I'd certainly have popped the question myself, early on. I really wish you the best, my dear, I really do. And nothing pleases me more than knowing that this time you can drive your own car home. I'll walk."

As they emerged from the restaurant, a free-lance street evangelist tried unsuccessfully to thrust a tract at Peckham.

"Brother, will you make a decision for Christ?"

"Why can't he make his own decisions?"

Peckham wasn't long in shaking his head in self-reproach, even shame, at that wiseacre retort. "Now will you believe what I said about human nature?" he said as he saw Binnie into her car for her solitary ride home. Sadly he walked the two miles back to his own house. Or rather Poppy's.

But a man wasn't a vulture. When he opened his eyes from the doze into which he had fallen under the sycamore at Dappled Shade, he saw the inmate he had come to visit making his way across the lawn from the main building. Dogwinkle was thinner since his nervous breakdown; not, as he himself readily professed, that he wasn't glad to be rid of a third of the chubby character he had once been. But his tweed suit was baggy, coat and pants both, and he had aged since the loss of the firm's three money-makers—Poppy McCloud's defection to belles-lettres and that of the others to rival publishers. He looked older than his fifty-two years. Only a takeover by an enormous media conglomerate had enabled him and Dearie to escape with anything like a whole hide; but the narrow escape from bankruptcy had so shaken Dogwinkle that a period of rest was indicated.

"So here we are picnicking again," he said in a rather shaky voice. "How long has it been since last time? Remember that beautiful July day so well."

"Little over three years. Well, four come this July. I hope you've brought your appetite with you. I remember the food here as great for institutions, making it so-so."

From a wicker hamper Peckham prestidigitated vichyssoise, deviled eggs and the mandatory fried chicken and potato salad, together with a bottle of cold rosé, which he poured into metal cups. It was not a question of heaping coals of fire on Dogwinkle's head. Being at least partly instrumental in making Dogwinkle and Dearie go belly-up had not proved the satisfaction Peckham had once thought it might be. Quite the contrary. Vengeance was the Lord's, and He could have it. It was not as sweet as advertised in the popular maxim. He was indeed sorry for Dogwinkle and enormously relieved to learn that he would be discharged in a few weeks. They lit into the food and the rosé heartily.

"Here's to the new book," Dogwinkle said. "How's it doing?"

"Triple the sales of *Sorry Scheme*. Of course it's only just out. Too early to tell."

"Do you see much of Poppy any more? I do hope she'll

finish the new novel soon. Of course we had her on a three-book contract, and we carry that asset with us into— I can hardly say it—Glamour Enterprises, but I do want to remain her editor."

"Over my dead body she'd switch. Anyway, I've never heard anything but praise for you from her. Look, do—"

Mother Nature strolled by, in one of her billowing silk gowns, and expected as usual to be complimented on the day.

"I've never seen anything like it for March," Peckham said. "Simply a jewel of a day."

"Thank you."

"Those clouds piling up in that blue sky. Like scoops of whipped cream."

"Well, *thank* you. I thought they were nice myself."

"Keep up the good work."

Peckham returned his attention to Dogwinkle.

"Do you see much of Mrs. DelBelly around? I understand she keeps a very sharp eye on the business affairs since that bustup with Hushnecker."

"I've seen her a few times yes, not just around the business office either. Seems to take pride in the place. Dr. Boondust—the chap I deal with—is more or less being groomed for administrative head, but I doubt he'll ever have the power that Hushnecker did. I hear he did manage to go south with quite a bundle—I mean got it stashed away somewhere before they caught up with him. They tell me you're quite matey with Mrs. Del. My God, this is good potato salad. Mark of the purist, leaving the jackets on. Where all the nourishment is. Potassium, isn't it? We and Poppy must all have lunch at the Algonquin one day soon. Glamour Enterprises can afford it."

"So that's what she's affectionately known as here. Mrs. Del. Has a kind of tycoon ring to it already. As though she's got the whole outfit pretty well bossed. Another splash of Tavel? I think you'll like those raspberry tarts."

TEN

"The thing about babies, you see, Mrs. Del, is their improbability."

This was far from chewing the rag properly so called. Had he unlearned everything about it in the intervening years? This was the art of conversation rearing its head again. He must put a tight rein on it, or he would find he had once again nuanced himself out of a good thing. He must not blow it this time. He needed more than ever the security in which to write his new book, this one to be a searing account of the breakup of a divorce. The greed of both parties, together with the avarice of wrangling lawyers, so hopelessly sinks all negotiations that settlement is impossible and the two combatants are forced to resume their intolerable coexistence. There was one other good reason for marriage to the now solidly single proprietor of Dappled Shade.

Peckham was not after all in such great psychic repair, taking everything into consideration. The fact that he looked from first to third before pitching the baseballs contrived out of wadded-up pages torn from literary periodicals with obtuse reviews, that had in the end not been deemed proof positive that he was going round the corner. Not so the most recent worsening: that he did throw the ball to first to pick off a runner threatening to steal second. Lodging at Dappled Shade might be obtained at a cut rate, or none at all, given himself as part owner of the place, owing to the twain being one flesh, with the time-honored "joint tenancy with right of survivorship," etc. The whirlpool baths and other therapeutic relaxations, the periodic sessions with Dr. Auslese, the calming strolls about the verdant grounds would all contribute to a quotidian rhythm he had found health-giving even his first time here as a simple convalescent, with no sign at all of any marbles missing. *Quotidian* had meant daily when he had first sprung the word on Mrs. DelBelly back then, and probably still did. He would make no such blunder again. He would talk United States, keeping a colloquial tongue in his head. He had half courted her then, with a rival on the scene in the shape, if one could call his physical composition that, of Dr. Hushnecker. To the merits she must have seen in him then could now certainly be added the advantage of comparison to someone who had turned out to be a mercenary rascal. Marriage could be foreseen as an almost certain outcome. Ah hoo boy.

"Binnie gave me a copy of your new book," Mrs. Del said, lowering herself into the chair he had drawn up for her under the spreading sycamore. A copy of the new book. Was the girl capable of any chicanery likely to queer this union? To—say it—prevent the acquisition of an Uncle Earl in at least partial charge of the purse

strings, and possibly the disposition of the inheritance itself?

"Yes, well, it was written in haste. There are some
things I would now . . ."

"I have been unable to read *The Ghastly Dinner Party,*
I'm sorry to say."

"Ah?"

"I mean I can't hold it. My hands hurt so I have to put
it down after five minutes." Possibly psychosomatic, a
somatically expressed disapproval of contemporary fiction
of a certain unsparing stripe? That was what Dr. Auslese
or Dr. Boondust would say. "So I can't say whether I like
it or not, my dear Earl." A ray of hope? "I have it with
everything I try to read. I don't know whether it's the
beginning of arthritis or not, but I have this pain in my
hands, both of them, right through here." She drew a
forefinger across the middle part of a palm and up into
the wrist. More than a ray of hope, a genuine beam of it!

"Well, we're going to take you right to the doctor and
have those hands examined."

"Our doctors here have medical degrees, of course, and
they're baffled by it. Can't figure out the cause."

"Then we're going to get you to a nerve specialist and
find out just exactly what the Sam Hill this is. I know a
good one in New York. Tops in his field. Connected with
Cornell Medical Center. I think I know what you've got,
but I'd like a second opinion."

"You do?"

Peckham nodded, closing his eyes slowly. With his elbows propped on the arms of his chair, he made a triangle

of his forefingers against pursed lips, striking the thoughtful attitude of a man who is a rock. Not just a brick, that would not be enough. He must be a rock. To that end he played the longest shot of his life.

"Does the worst discomfort come in the morning when you wake to find your hand oddly twisted, in a seemingly unconscious attempt to relieve the symptoms that have flared up in the night?"

"Why . . . yes."

Peckham nodded again, placing his forefingertips before his puckered lips a moment before continuing.

"Do you find it difficult to write, as difficult"—he gave a wryly affectionate smile—"as reading?"

"Yes."

"My dear, you have carpal tunnel syndrome."

Thank God for the *New York Times* health column. As an avid hypochondriac he read it religiously, looking for ailments within himself that he might have overlooked. There had been an article on carpal tunnel syndrome a few days before, on the details of which he was consequently almost letter-perfect. It is an almost totally unknown widely common disorder, caused by the compression of a nerve that runs through the hand into the wrist.

"Just like you've described to me," Peckham said. "The surgery it requires is a piece of cake. It's usually performed ambulatory. No hospitalization required at all, unless you might elect an overnight stay just to insure maximum care and comfort. I'll bet you dollars to doughnuts that's what you've got, my dear Nell."

It was. The New York doctor confirmed Peckham's diagnosis, sending Mrs. DelBelly into hitherto unimagined peaks of delight with her companion. He drove her to the New York hospital in one of her very own cars, a Cadillac brougham, brought flowers and fruit to her room, for she chose to stay overnight, and sat beside her bed stroking her bandaged hands, convinced there must be a God after all, and thanks to Him for carpal tunnel syndrome.

He sat close up to the bed while she talked of her operation, with an authority on carpal tunnel syndrome which she had by now wrested from Peckham's grasp and taken full possession of, which was fair enough, as she'd undergone the operation.

"Ackshy," she said, using that compression which was charming in her since it was epidemic among the young girls of college age on whose lips it was, however, irritating, "the neurological examination was worse. Pry as near to acapuncture as you can get without ackshy being that. The specialist who did it was nearly Chinese."

"I remember your telling me about it on the drive home when I took you to it. Stuck you with more needles than a cactus has."

"To see where the areas of numbness are, and how far up, you see."

"Ah."

"I realize now how long it was in coming on. The trouble I had twisting the caps off of jars of things and whatnot."

"You'll never have trouble twisting the caps off of jars of things again," he said tenderly, stroking the portions of her hands that were left available by the mummification. "Especially with Mrs. Spinelli around again." He went out on thin ice. "Or me. Give us—"

She rolled her gaze toward the door beyond which could

be heard the rustle and footscuffs of twenty-four-hour care.

"Those nurses are wonderful. I'd become one if I had it to do over again."

"Helping others is in your blood. It's your métier. That's why you own the best sanitarium in the state. Maybe the whole of New England," Peckham cried, bumbling like a smitten swain into the geographical error of including New York in it. To say nothing of picking runners off first and third. Was he coming unwrapped?

A nurse entered just then to look in, giving Mrs. Del no cause to break off her eulogy.

"We were just talking about you. Nurses in general, that is," she said to the blue-eyed ash blonde of whose other properties Peckham had already taken full account. "You're so good. Good at your job and good at heart. True angels of mercy."

"I agree," Peckham put in. "Recently I've had occasion for my own share of goodness and mercy, and I hope they don't follow me all the days of my life."

The nurse's face cracked in a smile rather broader than that of Mrs. DelBelly's, whose sharp eyes seemed to detect a flicker of amorous content in the glance exchanged between the other two.

"But Earl here remarked how you always ask patients to do things 'for you,' " she said mischievously. " 'Take these pills for me, would you? Eat a little of this custard for me.' Why do you do that?"

"I don't know," said Ash Blondie, bustling around a corner of the bed, tugging this and that to rights. "I guess it's that humoring note we like to strike. As though we know it's a nuisance, so the patient has to be coaxed. Would you move your chair back for me, Earl, so I can tidy up this side of the bed? Thanks."

Promptly on the nurse's departure, Peckham hitched his chair forward again and resumed caressing the accessible fingers, and the aborted advance of a moment ago to which the caresses were prelude.

"Give us a kiss," he said, and this time Nelly Del's arm reached up like a lariat around his neck and drew him down.

Mischance made it impossible fully to explore the significance of this lassoing just then, because at the moment their lips touched there was a gentle rap on the half-open door and Father Tooker stuck his head in. Unless it was precisely in this event that a shining augury lay. Because, seeing Peckham on deck, and perhaps sensing that he had caused a disengagement, Father Tooker shortened his visit to practically the duration of his prayer, which was O.K. of its kind and contained a minimum of lettuce, as Peckham thought of the hackneyed petitions that kept going, "Lettuce be thankful for this and lettuce find thy guiding hand in that, and lettuce continue to enjoy thy manifold blessings," and one thing and another, and before Father Tooker left, Mrs. Del invited both men thumpingly to tea on Saturday next. "I may not be able to pour, but that won't bother Earl, who'll want a martini anyway, or you, Jack Tooker, who'll be glad to settle for a sherry anytime."

"That compromise I'll be willing to make, Nell," said Father Tooker with the grin of the true heathen.

"Five o'clock, then."

So there they all three were in Nell's garden, around a white iron table under a spreading horse chestnut, with the martini and two sherries brought out by Mrs. Spinelli, who had just run away from her husband and family again and was back in service as housekeeper. She sprinted back in and back out again with a plate of cookies and cheese tidbits. There were four in the party in all if you counted the tabby, Samantha, in Mrs. Del's lap. She glanced at her wristwatch. "It's time for Hubert, the Rhinelanders' cat, to show up."

"Show up?" This from Peckham, glass at lip.

"Yes. He visits Samantha on weekends."

Peckham felt a chill of anxiety, then decided they were having their legs pulled by one with a store of humor previously unsuspected.

"Oh, Jack," she said to Father Tooker, "you missed a joke Earl pulled with the nurse the other night, just before you called. I should have told you then. Tell Jack, Earl— you know, about the goodness and mercy."

Peckham felt like a fool repeating it, but Father Tooker laughed like a fool on hearing it, adding that he might work it into a sermon sometime, if he might be permitted to steal it. Then with a sly glance at Peckham he changed the subject back to the cats and egged Nell to go on about the Rhinelanders' Hubert and his weekend visits.

"Oh, yes, it's quite true. Saturdays without fail, along about now. You'll presently see him moseying up along the road, to stay with Samantha here till Monday morning, when back he'll go. But I'm worried, or beginning to be. He should have turned up by now."

When at about a quarter to six she excused herself to slip into the house and telephone the Rhinelanders to see if there was anything amiss with Hubert, the tabby following in her wake, Peckham felt the same peculiar twinge of anxiety. Was she daft? Did she really believe this? Or was she having them on, as hoped? Her serious expression about it all would mean a deadpan delivery totally untypical of her. Japes and pranks were the farthest possible thing from her nature. He asked Father Tooker about it.

He cocked his head and shrugged, smiling more broadly now. "It's a story she keeps telling me. That's why I pressed her. I've never seen the other cat turn up, but then I've never been here on Saturday at this precise time before. You figure it out. We'll just have to wait and see, I guess. I'm just as curious as you."

They fell into a silence, and after a sip of his Dry Sack the reverend said, "You're a writer."

"Mea culpa," Peckham said, vexed with the good man for having provoked him into such an inane response. In any case, Nell must have spoken of him.

"Tried to write myself once, but . . ." Father Tooker parted his hands in a gesture pantomiming an effort come to nought. "Now getting out the Epiphany bulletin is about all I can manage, though I do polish off an article now and then for our denominational paper. I can't imagine your even knowing what that is," he added with a hollow laugh. "It's a question I'm sure you chaps are often asked, but who is your favorite writer?"

"There is no such thing. I mean the greatest composer, or the greatest artist—or one's favorite author. There are

225

great composers and artists, and one's favorite authors. But I've always especially liked Fitzgerald."

"Ah, yes. Some of those short stories." The reverend shook his head in helpless awe. Peckham found himself warming to the subject.

"My favorite single story of his would be the one called 'Absolution.' " In a way Peckham was probing an aching tooth here, that being the selection he would have chosen for a recent anthology entitled *I Wish I Had Written That*, to which he had fully expected to be tendered an invitation to contribute. He hadn't, but Poppy McCloud had. That still rankled. "Are you familiar with it?"

"Ah, yes. The priest and the boy. Read it several times."

That didn't absolve Father Tooker from hearing the comment Peckham would have supplied with his contribution—words themselves culled from an old classroom lecture remembered letter-perfect. He wet his whistle at the martini glass, cleared his throat and began.

" 'Absolution' relates a memorable intersection of two human crises, that of an adolescent lad chafing under a Catholic upbringing and a parish priest himself secretly crumbling under the weight of self-denial required by his faith. The latter's story is the more wrenching, being that of a mortal whose grace is unequal to the pressure put on it."

Father Tooker began to slump in his chair as if in inadvertent demonstration of the ordeal Peckham was relating. Also, his neck seemed to grow thinner inside a collar rather too large for him in any case, and he himself to shrink in a suit of clothes that also fit him too soon, as though he had recently lost weight, or in some predisposition to bagginess that was itself a modest form of sainthood. He rolled his watery gray eyes at Peckham as if mutely entreating him to desist, unless it was a plea to spare him nothing in the way of relevance.

"Once met, Father Schwartz is never forgotten," Peckham in any case went remorselessly on, as though this lecture were a foretaste of the sermons Father Tooker and Nell Del between them were conspiring that Father Tooker would preach Peckham once Peckham had been dragged into the fold, following a marriage for which he ambivalently pined in a drive toward self-crucifixion of his own. "For the climax offers one of the most heartbreaking glimpses of the disintegration of a man in modern fiction. Ostensibly cued by the boy's confession to pronounce the usual benediction, he begins to rave insanely of the pleasurable world for which all his life he has inwardly yearned, and to which we know from his own private fantasies the lad is himself inevitably tending. 'When a lot of people get together in the best places things go glimmering,' the man of God babbles as he collapses to the floor."

Father Tooker seemed to mumble something inarticulate himself as he slumped farther down in his chair, as though he might slide out of it altogether onto the grass, and with his right hand he made a faint gesture, again indecipherable as to whether he meant thereby that Peckham should stop or should go on, spare him nothing. The man of the cloth could hardly have divined that Peckham was writhing under a similar lash, as one basically excluded from the worldly renown he had craved and been denied.

As it were, neither was to get off Scott-free. Ah hoo boy.

"The story can be equally moving to believer and unbeliever. For the one, it is a graphic reminder of what must be renounced if one is to join the saints in glory; for the other, a piercing object lesson of the flesh mortified in vain. It is all, in the end, for nothing."

Father Tooker seemed on the verge of really executing his threatened reenactment of Father Schwartz's own collapse by winding up a crumpled heap on the ground. But he pulled himself together and straightened up, reaching to the table for his sherry. He had a question.

"I've often puzzled over one thing in that story. The title. Who, then, is absolved, and by whom?"

"Both I think, by the author. Himself our most shining chronicler of that world where a lot of people get together in the best places and things go glimmering."

The priest nodded. "I can naturally appreciate that better than you. Being an Episcopalian, I'm not celibate by requirement, only by choice. I'm"—he threw his arms out—"well, hell, just a bachelor. Just another bachelor. Which from what Nell tells me you've been yourself, but without any of the, ahem, denials I've had to elect by virtue of my position. But I think you can appreciate what I appreciate in the story, and why it has always cut close to the bone for me." He smiled, and with it the black coat seemed a little less baggy and his collar a trifle closer to fitting him. "Whether I shall at last join the saints in glory is not for me to say, but I like to think I haven't mortified the flesh in vain. And in a community like this, well, I do enjoy some of the best places where people get together and things go glimmering."

With that he looked toward the house, from which Nell was again emerging, the tabby once more traipsing along behind her.

"Hubert is sick," she announced. "That's why he can't make it this weekend."

"Ah," the two men said, each wondering what the other might be secretly thinking. Ought the woman all along to be housed in her own sanitarium? There had up to now been no signs . . . not the least clue . . .

They watched as Samantha continued on toward the road, turned right, and walked along its shoulder till she disappeared from view behind a row of trees.

"Where is she going?" Peckham asked.

"To the Rhinelanders'," Nell answered. "She knows Hubert's sick, so she's going to *his* place to spend the weekend instead. She heard me on the telephone just now. They do switch around like that once in a while. Well. Another sherry? Martini? I'll call Mrs. Spinelli."

ELEVEN

As an Episcopalian, Nelly DelBelly knew what *the* Epiphany was—a season of three weeks on the denominational calendar, beginning January 6, to celebrate the manifestation of the divine nature of Christ to the Gentiles as represented by the visit of the Magi. It was also the name of the local congregation to which she belonged, and contributed. But she probably didn't know that *an* epiphany, a lower-case, or pop, epiphany, was a secular derivative of the doctrine now used by moderns from SoHo to L.A. to indicate any sudden intuitive revelation. Currently the mods made a verb of it—"We epiphanized about each other"—which drove Peckham crazy, in the way that *prioritized* did. Well, sir, he had an epiphany as he awoke with a start from a light doze he had fallen into while seated beside Nell in her favorite pew at the Church of the Epiphany, into whose membership she had been striving to draw him since she had become Mrs. Peckham. He experienced both the snooze and the epiphany in the course of a sermon being delivered by Jack Tooker's young curate, currently being tried out as a sandman and doing

231

a bang-up job. Whether Tooker had ever delivered that sermon on whether God had humor, Peckham never learned.

Manderley dreams rarely occurred in daytime naps, but this one did, and in the course of it, or eerily timed with his arousal from it by a nudge from his wife, came the blinding realization that Florence Bates, who played the woman to whom Joan Fontaine was paid companion, Mrs. DelBelly, and Margaret Dumont, the similarly shaped actress who served as a foil for Groucho Marx in so many films, were one and the same. The real epiphany was the delayed realization that it had all been subconsciously in Peckham's mind from the first of the rag-chewing attempts in the bosky gardens of Dappled Shade, particularly the linkage between La Dumont and La DelBelly. Oh, not so much in the matter of their size; their Junoesque figures stirred associations to which no guilt need adhere once you thought of them, flatteringly, as Junoesque. It was the question of humor. Groucho had sworn to his dying day, and at least once on public television, that Margaret Dumont had never understood one word of the material in the scripts, even the famous line in the battle scene in *Duck Soup*, "Remember you're fighting for this woman's honor, which is more than she ever did!" Neither, to all appearances, did Nelly comprehend the majority of Peckham's quips, the quality of which was itself not the point.

Guilt rocked Peckham when he had the epiphany—at Epiphany, on Epiphany Sunday of all days—as his head jerked erect with a snap that might easily have netted him a whiplash judgment against the curate. Remorsefully, he tried to concentrate on the rest of the sermon, with a vow that in the future he would more affectionately respect Nell's qualities as a churchwoman. And as a Latter Day Dadaist, what difference did it make where you were? But presently he found his attention wandering and his head swiveling slowly to the left where he knew Binnie was sitting, no doubt cajoled to church by her husband as Peckham was by his wife. His neck took another snap back, this time lateral. He had caught Dempster's own eye glowering his way. If his displeasure was worse than usual it was because he had recently been burned on pork bellies, not because Peckham had been giving him any further cause for jealousy.

He had another lower-case epiphany. Dempster reminded him of Beethoven. That was owing solely to the similarity in foreheads. Beethoven had a brow like a thunderclap, and so did Dempster, at least when directed at Peckham. Dempster bruxed when in the presence of Peckham. Meaning he ground his teeth. It's evidently the word for it. He was no doubt bruxing now. Peckham for his part could boast one unalloyedly pure thought this morning. He thanked God Dempster was here in church and not at the Sunday-morning Al-Anon meeting at Dappled Shade. It meant Binnie was on the wagon. Peckham breathed a silent prayer that it would remain so.

Peckham's admittance into the household of faith came to pass in this wise. He sinned that grace might abound. In the hour of thoughtless youth he had blithely jabbered, "Having a wife and a mistress both is like having your bread buttered on both sides." He found out later what

233

he meant without knowing it at the time—namely that it's more of a mess than you had bargained for. The epigram was to remain durable for future use—with the adjunct appended.

Nell and Peckham gave a small dinner party to celebrate their first anniversary, with Dempster giving a toast on which he must nearly have choked. He grinned like a stuffed lynx when wringing Peckham's hand in congratulation, with a force that threatened carpal tunnel syndrome for Peckham. Then he bruxed for a while. And Binnie fell off the wagon with the champagne on which she joined in the toast. Peckham steered her into a corner and said, "Look, don't do this, dear. One was O.K., but this is four. I'm counting if you don't."

"What, the money?"

"I'll let that pass." He went on seriously. "Hypnotism sometimes helps. Not often. Very seldom in fact, I gather. But sometimes. As it does with cigarettes."

"That's not my curse, luckily. Look, are you enjoying life in the tub of butter you've landed in? Are you still cutting the pages in the books in the library, or did you finish that on your honeymoon? Congratulations."

"I won't dignify anything that cynical with a reply. But getting back to the hypnotism. I know someone who's practiced it on a smoker, with fairly good results. Not glowing, but good."

"Who?"

"Me."

Binnie opened her mouth in a soundless gasp, then let go with a laugh. "Of course! You and the Svengali bit. I

234

remember your telling me you had that power the first time we met, right here. Sitting over there."

"No, I didn't tell you, you told me. But what I've said is true. What could we lose by trying it?"

"I'm game, what the hell. But where? When?"

"Here. Next Thursday. Nell's going into the city on a shopping spree and wants to stay in my apartment for a couple of days. Alone. Makes a great point of not liking a man tagging along when she's cutting a swath through Bergdorf's and Bonwit's. Makes her nervous to have him watching her try things on. Also, she wants to meet an old lady friend from Toledo who'll be in New York then. Take in a few art galleries and one thing and another. High school chum she keeps up with. So we'll be alone. House to ourselves."

"What about Mrs. Spinelli?"

"Her day off."

"All right. What can we lose?"

That was soon seen. She arrived at the appointed hour, two in the afternoon, looking very spruce in a red linen suit in which she stretched out obligingly on a parlor sofa. But she got the giggles when Peckham began swinging his wristwatch back and forth and telling her she was going to sleep, sleep, sleep. Finally she reached up with both arms and drew him down onto the sofa, not quite on top of her, but not quite beside her either. He proved powerless against that ripe red mouth and the cloud of scent in which he likewise found his senses reeling. He felt her tongue stroking the underside of his upper lip in a kiss the exact initiation of which he wasn't quite sure of, except that, she being the aggressor, hers was the sin of commission while his was one of omission, consisting as it did of a failure to resist. He had a lunatic vision of Father Tooker making that precise distinction to Nell in a learned exegesis of this iniquity when it all came out. "This beats drinking," she breathed, in a fragrance of recently discarded Juicy Fruit gum and perfume whose commingled intimacies further crazed his senses. "We've had this date for a long time," she panted, though as the man it was he who should have been gasping that echo from *Streetcar*. She ground her loins against his in a fever he quite reciprocated, feeling more and more like a Stanley Kowalski playing truant from a platonic marriage. As though exercising some kind of local autonomy of which his mind distantly approved, his hand found its way under her skirt and traveled up her thigh until it felt the strand of elastic it was looking for. The rustle of clothing made him almost miss another sound coming from the far end of the room— almost but not quite. There it was again. He unlocked himself from their embrace and twisted upward into a sitting position, at the same time turning his head toward the foyer. Through the half-open double doors he saw a ghost standing on the bottom step of a flight of stairs just visible beyond them. It was Mrs. Spinelli in her flannel bathrobe, her hair down around her face. He popped to his feet while Binnie, having sat up long enough to take in what had roused his attention, lay down again with her face hidden under a cushion.

"Mrs. Spinelli. Aren't you off today?"

"No. I been under the weather. Touch of the flu or

something. So I thought I'd better stay home and spend the day in bed. That maybe what you'd care to be doing?" she added, and went on into the kitchen mumbling something about hot water and lemon.

"Jesus Christ," Peckham said.

Binnie rose and began to tidy herself for a quick flight.

"Couldn't you have made sure? I mean she's got a lip on her, besides which you never know what she's thinking. I've always found her scary. Why does she work live-in anyway, five miles from her own home?"

"She can't stand her husband. I think she's discovered separation is fashionable. And she's somehow got this idea that day work is beneath her."

"I'm getting out of here. I just hope she didn't recognize me. Hate to leave you with this can of worms, but it really is yours to deal with, isn't it, in all fairness?"

"I guess." It was peanut-butter time again. Imaginary wads of it mired his tongue against the roof of his mouth. The more so when, Binnie flown, he went into the kitchen to seek executive clemency from Mrs. Spinelli.

"Appearances are deceiving, and this little—"

"I know," she said from the sink, where she was squeezing out the juice of a lemon.

"With all our scientific know-how and medical progress, few people realize the value of hot water and lemon juice. There's an instinctive folk wisdom about it. My parents always went for it at the first sign of— Look. This is not what it seems. Spot of the old slap-and-tickle," he babbled, as though this were a brittle British drawing room comedy, of which one scene happened to be played in the

237

kitchen, or below stairs. "We're old friends, and we'll say no more about this, right?"

"I hope so."

"Just one of those things."

"I'm sure we can work something out."

What did she mean? Peckham wondered later, for he had sensed something ominous in her voice. Was she going to blackmail him in some way? And in what way?

He now lived with the same daily dread of exposure that had dogged his relationship with Poppy. It was anxiety of a vastly different sort, of course, but similar in the fear of his peace being blown sky-high at any time. He could hardly face Mrs. Spinelli, who remained nerve-rackingly inscrutable with her little secret. What had she meant by "work something out"? At last the other shoe dropped.

"That club you belong to," she said one afternoon when the two were again alone in the kitchen, this time with Peckham pitching in with more than his usual gusto in helping with dinner preparations. Indeed, his continued pleasure in cooking at least half the evening meals was what made it possible to rub along with no more than a single servant. "The country club."

"Rolling Acres."

"Yes. It must be nice there. I'd like to become a member. Not for myself so much, or my husband either, but my two children. Nick and Anna. I believe you've met them."

"Yes. Lovely young people," Peckham said, against his better recollection that Nick had at least one car-theft attempt to his credit as a juvenile delinquent, and his total ignorance of Anna.

238

"It would be nice for them to have the privileges that go with that. And mingling with the best people. That always means a lot."

Peckham's blood froze at the realization of what she was demanding as the price of her silence. Put her and Mr. Spinelli, an electrical contractor, up for membership in one of the most exclusive country clubs in the county. He went sick at the thought. To have asked for a thousand dollars, even five, would have been less ghastly than this, granted that it would have entailed the further deception of siphoning from a checking account on which Nell kept a sharp eye. Perhaps some sort of bookkeeping finagle would work. The alternative would have been a loan shark certain to send a few mouth breathers around to dust you off for payment arrears.

"I think the membership is full. Perhaps another time . . ."

"No it isn't. I've made ink wearies."

Ink wearies. Peckham screwed his face up in puzzled thought. Ink wearies. Of course. Inquiries. It was how people pronounced it who were determined the accent was on the first syllable.

"You've made ink wearies?"

"Yes. They're taking. They've got openings. The Fevershams, I'm sure you know them, I used to be in service there, they just got in. I keep up. You put a prospect up and then have a reception where we're displayed to the membership committee, who would then pass on us. That's the routine."

"But a reception at which the prospective member would

239

be serving—" His knees went weak at the very notion. "You can see the paradox yourself."

"Right. I would be passing the committee members cheese dreams they knew I had made myself. Many's the compliments I've had from them before. That's democracy at work. And my bacon wrapped around water chestnuts, they flip over them."

"I'll see what I can do." Peckham answered limply, and tottered out of the kitchen.

"Thank you."

He went out for a walk, scarcely knowing what streets he scuttled along, turning corners at random and dropping into a tavern for a quick one here and there. He found himself doing that increasingly as his problem gnawed away at him. Tension mounted, as in the heart of Earl Peckham these unforeseen events formed a tightening knot within his troubled breast. It was as if—God, not that one again—it was as if the air darkened with evil birds coming home to roost. Not a hackneyed phrase, but he was entangled in it. He was living a lie, he was a whited sepulcher. He had made his bed, now he must lie in it, racked with the certainty that he couldn't lie out of it. A bed short-sheeted by none other than himself. As he had sown, so would he reap. Sleep knitted up the raveled sleeve of care. But what would knit up the raveled sleeve of sleep? He tossed and turned, knowing that each day got through postponed the inevitable: the time when, Mrs. Spinelli's patience having run out, he must with a straight face make her outrageous proposal to Nell. Because they would have to put the Spinellis up for membership in Rolling Acres together. If they didn't, would Mrs. Spinelli really spill the beans? It was hard to believe she would. Yet the possibility was impossible to ignore. The risk of marital hell and high water would be worse than the ordeal that remained its alternative.

He plucked up his courage to take the plunge. But first there was a preparatory move. A sort of curtain raiser to the main drama.

He picked his time carefully. He and Nell had settled down to their evening drinks, a sherry for her and a martini for him. It was Mrs. Spinelli's day off again, he had fixed both the drinks and a favorite appetizer, salmon roe on slices of cold chicken, and they were pleasantly alone, together. And in the library, so much cozier than the main living room.

"Nell," he said, "I've made a decision."

"For what?"

"For Christ."

This flamboyantly evangelical way of putting it, more revival meeting than high Anglican, was so unfamiliar to a suburban Episcopalian, that for a moment she didn't know what he meant. Then its full import struck her—the realization of her fondest wish, namely, that he join the church—struck her with such force that she rose and went over to embrace Peckham, spilling half her sherry in her joy.

"Oh, Earl! I'm so glad. It's what I've wanted. You know that."

"I know, my dear."

She dithered about for a moment, walking around the room and clasping and unclasping her hands in an access of delight. It was a dream come true. She was beside

PETER DE VRIES

herself. Rarely had she looked so forward to anything. Seldom had she been in a heaven so seventh. "And Jack Tooker will be so glad. Let's call him. Right away!"

"Now, now, just a minute. Let's not make too big a deal of this. I mean, I speak as a lapsed Presbyterian after all, so it'll only be a question of having my membership transferred from back home in Wyoming. And I've been baptized, so there needn't be any of that."

"You'd still have to be confirmed. That's what we have, you know."

"But not subjected to instruction or any of that," he bleated. "I could tell Jack Tooker a thing or two about the history of theology. Ask Jack. He'll say the same thing. So let's just say I'm joining Epiphany."

"Swell. But I will tell Jack soon. He'll be tickled to a fairly well."

Peckham waited three days before putting the proposition to which this was preparation. They were at dinner, a chicken casserole in white wine that he had often fixed, and he knew that beyond the closed swinging door Mrs. Spinelli was listening as she partook of her own share. Peckham lowered his voice only slightly, so that she might catch what he was saying and know that he had kept his part of the bargain.

"Dear, Mrs. Spinelli has given some evidence that she'd like to become a member of the country club. Oh, not for her and Mr. Spinelli so much as for the children. What say we offer to propose them?"

Nell lowered an overflowing fork from her open mouth back to her plate.

242

"Are you out of your mind?"

"No, why?" He tried to seem unruffled as he poured himself some more white Burgundy.

"But it's preposterous. They wouldn't fit in. And the members would be shocked. At the very idea."

"Why? We mustn't as Christians look down on anyone."

"Christians, are you mad? What's that got to do with it?"

"Everything. Our Lord enjoins us to charity, love for all our fellow creatures. Doesn't he?"

"But he didn't belong to a country club. They didn't have them then. I mean . . ." She had picked up her fork but again lowered it, this time with a clatter, and then threw up her hands. "I simply. You simply. I can't imagine what's gotten into you." The resemblance to Margaret Dumont was so startling that he had a fleeting delusion that he was Groucho Marx and would any moment rise and continue his part of the dialogue loping around the table. "I simply can't imagine. The Spinellis at Rolling Acres." She rolled her eyes as though lifting them up unto the hills, whence came her help. "Oh, let's not spoil a good dinner with a conversation like this. Joining the church is one thing, but getting religion, I mean next you'll be on the floor like a Holy Roller. Really, Earl, you ought to pull yourself together and take things within reason. The Spinelli family isn't a really intact one anyway, else why would she take a live-in situtation five miles from home."

"O.K., we'll discuss it another time." Peckham was

satisfied that Mrs. Spinelli had heard enough and was now honor-bound to call off her dogs. It was the mistress who was the roadblock, not the master.

He dropped the subject, but that didn't prevent Nell from bringing it up again. Something about it all had been gnawing at her. Struck her as fishy.

"Why did Mrs. Spinelli put this up to you and not me? Why are you always having brief whispered discussions behind closed doors which are broken off when I open them?" The syntax provided Peckham a surrealist image of portals unhinged as she regally bore down on them, but little relief from the crisis apparently enveloping them anew. Nell was having an epiphany of her own. "There's something between you two, isn't there?"

"Nell." Peanut-butter time again. "There's no one but you. I swear."

"You mean—? Oh, my God." Again like something from an inferior work of fiction. He had never written "You mean—?" and here it was running him down like a truck.

"So. No one but me. You swear. When a man swears that, it means he's had an affair going, or at least a canoodle, but there's 'no one but' the wronged person *really*. Oh!"

Peckham had a counterepiphany. Granted Nell had a suspicion on the boil, it was far, far better to have her think it was Mrs. Spinelli than learn it was Binnie. There was a corollary inspiration that might just complete salvation. A Mrs. Spinelli compromised was a Mrs. Spinelli with her leverage gone. That was one thing. Then, an ego suddenly buoyed by advances on the master's part might be another factor making her relent, to the extent of causing her to forget poor Binnie altogether. It was a long shot but it was worth taking—was, in fact, necessary, given the present muddle. Helping Mrs. Spinelli polish some silver in the kitchen supplied a conceivable occasion for making her a fellow wrongdoer. Truth to tell, she was in middle years still quite toothsome, with the trim figure, full mouth and dark eyes instantly appreciated at that housewarming way back then, when her views on God and humor had proved stunning. And slipping an arm around her waist, once he had maneuvered closer to her at the counter where they were buffing away at the silver, seemed not all that more outlandish than picking runners off first and third.

"Give us a kiss."

"Why, Mr. Peckham," she said, trying to wriggle free, with a giggle rather than a flash of anger. That in itself instantly telegraphed to Peckham that he was home and dry.

"You're quite an attractive woman, you know. I've always thought so. And the way you—how shall I put it?—walk."

"Thank you, but . . . we shouldn't."

"Perhaps you're right. We're mad. You have to be the strong one. End this thing before it goes any further. That perfume you're wearing, and what you've done to your hair."

"You've noticed. You like it this way?"

"Yes. Shortening hair always makes a woman look

younger. Not that you . . . But you're right. You've got to be sane for both of us. And I'm sorry the country club thing didn't work out. Under all those protests I was secretly thinking of the sight of you around the pool, of finding you there. I suppose deep down I knew it was danger."

"You're a real rascal, aren't you. A regular Casanova. But you're right. One of us has got to use his head."

It was then that Nell walked in.

"So!" she said. "I thought I'd heard enough out there to understand what was going on in here," freely admitting her own transgression as an eavesdropper. It was as though they were all rotten, on the highest social level. "And now I've seen enough to make me understand *everything*. You're through here," she finished, and marched out trailing some confusion as to who exactly had been fired. Maybe both of them.

But of course it was Mrs. Spinelli who packed and left, with three weeks' pay, leaving Peckham stuck with an admittedly deserved but totally unexpected outcome to his fling with Binnie. On Mrs. Spinelli's departure, that very day, there were enough tasty leftovers (Christ, how he hated that word *tasty*) from a potpie he'd baked the day before to furnish them with a dinner for two. Or rather two dinners, because Nell took hers up to her room. His own appetite being nil, he took a snifter three-quarters filled with brandy up to his own room and stretched out on the bed there to think things through. At bedtime, roughly ten o'clock around here, there were footsteps in the hall outside the closed door, then the door opened and Nell stood there.

"Get out."

"Of the house?"

"No, I mean sleep on the sofa. You're going to sleep on the sofa tonight."

He lay there in utter amazement, not too much blurred by drink to experience that. This was It. Here was a man whose life had been dedicated to the quest for subtlety, a concomitant of which would naturally be an abhorrence of the trite, being told to sleep on the sofa like a Rotarian whose peccadillo at a Chicago hardwaremen's convention had been discovered by a wife with combs in her hair. The most predictably threadbare turn in the most hack-neyed imaginable merry-marital-mixup of a television sit-com. He drew himself up to his full height, to the extent that that can be done lying down, and said, "I rather imagine I shan't do any such thing at all."

"Down."

"Darling, our first quarrel," he said, to rub salt into his gaping wound with the ultimate reductio ad absurdum.

"Down." This time she pointed an arm toward the living room where the banal sofa lay in readiness.

"But don't you see how meaningless this is. This is my regular room *anyway*, one to which I might conceivably have been banished, yes, if we occupied the same bed. So you don't have to do any more banishing."

"It's my bedroom in my house. And I don't want to sleep with you so much as on the same floor tonight."

"I still adhere to my point of view."

"In that case I'll call the police."

"On what charge?"

"Trespassing. The place is in my name."

"Oh, all right."

His compliance turned out to offer the quickest and best emergence from an untidy situation, running on roughly the same transfer-of-guilt lines as in the case of his blowup with Poppy. Finding him there in the morning, blanketless and wakeful, indeed red-eyed, made her realize the severity of her response. She too had overreacted—completing the dismal round of bromides into which they had been uncontrollably sucked. For Peckham's part, the battle itself had generated emotions curiously convertible into—yes, sexual desire. He blew up the coals of animosity into just the tiniest flare of a spat, however, before expressing contrition and asking forgiveness for a canoodle with a housemaid as commonplace, if it came to that, as exile to the sofa. "Sleep" had been a series of snoozes in which he'd dreamt of Cardinal Richelieu, wombats, that sort of thing. The morning sky was the pink of boiled ham, but it had nothing to do with him.

"If I'd known this was what Christians were like, I might have thought twice about joining their organized ranks," he said, and rose, drawing about him the bathrobe he had worn in lieu of night covers. A sidelong glance indicated that he was making ground as the injured party.

"I'm sorry," she said, and half turned to him in her chair. The tautness of her blue silk robe emphasized the really firm arc of her flanks, as well as the never-doubted opulence of her breasts. He came over, pitifully trailing the thong of his robe, which he had let come loose again, and laid a hand on her shoulder, tousling her hair with the other.

"It's all right. I'm sorry too. Much sorrier of course. The whole thing was too silly right from the beginning. I blame myself."

Nell rose to his embrace. Thus did hostility again move in its mysterious ways its wonders to perform. A marriage in name only lay in fragments at their feet, never to be pieced together again. The union was consummated that night, in the bower he had first seen as just another guest trooping through the house on a grand tour.

So it came out well all around, even for poor Mrs. Spinelli. Her feminine pride was indeed so bolstered by Peckham's advances that her having to leave was cherished as proof that she was still attractive to men. A breath of scandal gave her a certain kudos in that particular time and place. The new housekeeper, named Mrs. Grundy of all things, was chosen to guarantee no threat of amorous disarray at that address. The new will ultimately drawn up, though not for a few years, provided for a joint division between Peckham and Binnie, satisfactory even to Dempster, who for the most part has stopped bruxing in Peckham's presence. All that, provided Aunt Nell predeceases them, which has become laughably unlikely. If fate has another chronology in store, the estate is to be divided equally between the church and an assortment of specified charities. If Binnie and Dempster have any children, the inheritance is diverted to them.

Binnie has remained temperant, as has Poppy with cigarettes—with an occasional expected lapse. Poppy continues to turn out novels that reach the bestseller lists, but by no means the top—Peckham's tutelage has proved too durable for that. They are a blend of her old viscerality and the more cerebral element Peckham has instilled into her work. Dogwinkle is happy serving as her editor.

Peckham works away at his old pace, in at least material security. He can't help thinking his stuff might be better if his past had only been worse. As an artist, he can hardly forgive his parents for the halcyon childhood they afforded him, and secretly envies successful rivals their professedly gruesome beginnings. Childhood adversity is apparently what puts fuel in the creative engine, or demons to work out of the system vicariously. If his parents had only given him a broken home by divorcing, or made the one they had a hell by fighting or falling into drunken stupors, leaving him to fend for himself at a tender age, his adult work might have possessed greater resonance. In a series of television interviews with writers of current renown, one author had related with tears in his eyes, and this on an educational network, how his father had put rocks in his diapers to keep him from climbing out of his crib. Just something like that might have done it for Peckham, enabled him to make that final ascent into excellence. But he keeps plugging along with what he has. Now and then he is shaken to find a work of genuine literary merit on the bestseller lists. But he gets through such days with a little extra Bordeaux from a fine cellar, and the reminder that nothing in this world always works the way it is supposed to, nothing is consistent. And, of course, to-morrow is another day. He has abandoned the previously planned novel for one tentatively called *A Shred of De-*

cency. The title alone indicates a new mellowness, just the suggestion of optimism, the belief or at least hope that his species is not as totally unredeemable, or fate as utterly inclement, as previously thought.

One day on a solitary rambling gad about New York he saw an old dream fulfilled—a mass display of a work of *his* in a bookstore. But the pleasure was short-lived. Almost simultaneously with the glimpse of it came the realization that he had wandered into one of those discount outlets that specialize in publishers' remainders. This overstock of *The Ghastly Dinner Party*, standing in a solid block on the floor, was being unloaded at 98¢. As Peckham saw it, he could do one of two things. He could lie down on it, with his arms outstretched in a cruciform position, and say, "Father, it is finished." Or he could hang about for a bit and see whether any browsers were drawn to it and even any purchases resulted. There were hopeful signs that the forbidding rectangle had already been nibbled away at. The sides were uneven, the surface far from smooth. And sure enough, in the course of ten minutes or so while he hovered about pretending to browse himself, two people bought the book, the second a woman who took three copies. Obviously someone who had already read it and liked it enough to be giving it away as a present—Christmas was just around the corner. The impulse to dart forward and offer his signature was stemmed aborning; embarrassment would have outweighed satisfaction. And as for the store's remainder of his remainders, Dogwinkle's myth about the unreturnability of inscribed copies had long ago been exploded as such. All in all, the incident was not as bad as might otherwise have been the case, even had its bracing side. A brief flareup of the now all but unrecurring Manderley dream, a few days of picking runners off first and third, and it was forgotten, gathered into the ever-accumulating stream of yesterdays. Of years in which he rereads many of his own favorites, some of *them* picked up as bargains in remainder charnels, or in used-book shops because they are out of print, a fate hardly more palatable. He rereads on long winter evenings before the fire, or golden summer Sunday afternoons in the gazeboed garden.

The Rhinelanders' cat, Hubert, still indeed comes to visit Nell's tabby, Samantha, on weekends. And of course the Peckhams have weekend guests of their own, all Nell's friends. He hasn't any. He never has had any friends, only lovers, and thus her circle becomes increasingly important as the years roll on. They keep the old Village pied-à-terre for occasional, in fact frequent, trips into New York, shopping, theater going, museum attending, and the like. They often lunch at the Plaza, which she is fond of, but when he goes into town alone it's always the Algonquin. By force of hard-dying habit, or perhaps just lingering illusion, he strains to catch scraps of the conversation bubbling around him—as no doubt do many out-of-town-ers—in the hope of hearing snatches of the wit for which the hotel is traditionally famous. Of everything on which he has eavesdropped as he sipped his martini or partook of his meal, he has heard only one thing he truly wishes he had said. A man at the next table remarked to his lady companion, "My last book sold a hundred and ninety-seven thousand copies."

He wishes he had said that.

But thinking as much over his solitary drink was never more than a pleasantry devised for his own rueful amusement, a characteristic stroke of reflection summarizing a life best described by the word he probably hated most in the English language—*bittersweet*. For Peckham never really believed in either the orgiastic future or the triumphal entry, only a reasonably enjoyable journey with a thousand modest destinations but no smashing arrival. He is like all of us, organically programmed to be both predator and prey, an arrangement we are powerless not to visit on our fellows. He takes satisfaction in having quite lived by his stoic creed: give what you can and take what comes. Concession not freely given is in the end forcibly exacted anyway. For we are all swimmers ephemerally buoyed by what will engulf us at the last; still dreaming of islands though the mainland has been lost; swept remorselessly out to sea while we spread our arms to the beautiful shore.

Catalog

If you are interested in a list of fine Paperback
books, covering a wide range of subjects
and interests, send your name and address,
requesting your free catalog, to:

McGraw-Hill Paperbacks
11 West 19th Street
New York, N.Y. 10011